Summer Love

A SUMMERS IN SEASIDE AND SEASONS OF LOVE CROSSOVER
BOOK TWO

C.L. COLLIER

Summer Love

It's bound to be a fantastic weekend in Seaside, Oregon with my closest friends. Not only are we staying at the adorable Sandy Shore Inn, we're also excited to attend the Seaside Festival's Book Signing Event. After all, we librarians love our books...

Which also brings us to the local bookstore, Booked at the Beach.

I'm immediately attracted to the cozy little shop... and to the hot, sexy man working behind the counter.

When Garrick shows up at the book signing's VIP dinner and is seated at the same table, I feel a rush of excitement. We quickly discover we have more in common than just a love for books.

Things between Garrick and me progress quickly, but is it too good to be true? After all, he lives in Oregon and I live several hours away in Port Townsend. How can we make this work?

Then, he lets me in on his little secret...

Editing by Susan Soares, SJS Editorial Services

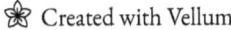 Created with Vellum

I dedicate this book to my daughter. You're amazing.

Summer

Chapter 1

Welcome to Seaside.

I roll the car windows down and let the wind whip my hair as I drive into the city limits of Seaside, Oregon. It's been a long day of driving—a little over four hours—and I'm ready to start my week of vacay at the beach with my best girlfriends from college. We get together every summer for a fun, relaxing girls weekend, and this year, we've chosen the small coastal town as our destination.

I slow to a stop, surprised by the long line of traffic. I suppose I shouldn't be surprised, though, considering the Seaside Festival brings a high volume of tourists to the town this time of year. After all, that's the sole reason we've chosen to come. There are several fun activities to partake in while the festival is going on, but what has *really* drawn us here is the Seaside Festival's book signing event, which is featuring several of our favorite authors. Not only are my friends and I avid readers, we're also all librarians. Books are our lives.

"*Traffic ahead. You're still on the quickest route,*" my navigation alerts me.

"Gee, thanks. I couldn't tell," I say sarcastically.

I look at the map and see that I'll arrive at the Sandy Shore Inn in seven minutes. Not too bad. I'm excited to get there, considering I'm the last of my friends to arrive. They've already checked into our rooms at the B&B, and they're currently sitting outside on the deck, enjoying the view with a bottle of wine. I know because they called to see how far out I was about ten minutes ago.

The friends I'm meeting all live in the Greater Seattle area. Michelle drove down from Woodinville and picked Penny up in Federal Way, then they stopped to get Angela in Olympia on their way. Since I'm the only one who lives all the way over on the Olympic Peninsula and took a completely different route to get to Seaside than they did, I drove alone. The four of us met when we attended school at Pacific Northwest University, or PNWU. We graduated seven years ago and have made it a point to get together at least once a year ever since. We used to get together more regularly, but it's become more difficult since they all got married. Penny has a one-year-old daughter now, and Angela's expecting her first baby in December. I'm the only single one in the bunch.

After inching along through traffic, I finally make it to the other side of town and arrive at the Sandy Shore Inn exactly when my navigation predicted I would. The bed and breakfast looks just as it's pictured online. An old Victorian home with a stately turret and wrap-around porch, which according to the online photos, overlooks the beach in the back, about a football field's length away from the Pacific Ocean. I've been looking forward to coming here ever since Michelle suggested this was the place we should stay.

I park next to Michelle's white Camry, then send a text to our group chat to let my friends know I've arrived. Angela replies just as I open the trunk to retrieve my suitcase, telling me that they're still sitting on the back porch, but she'll come inside to meet me. I throw my phone into my purse, get my suitcase, close the trunk, and lock my car, then head toward the entrance of the inn.

The smell of jasmine and patchouli fills the air as I walk in the house. It's lovely. So far, I love everything about this place. The foyer is grand, with a check-in desk front and center. No one is working there at the moment, but that's okay since I don't need to check in. My friends have already done that, and Angela and I are sharing a room. I look to my right and see a gift shop, which looks to be filled with all sorts of New Age things. I'll have to check it out later.

"Summer!" I turn to see Angela walking into the foyer from somewhere in the back of the house.

"Hey!" We walk toward each other and hug. "It's so good to see you!"

"Same! I'm so glad you're here," she says as we pull apart from each other.

"Me, too. This place looks amazing. And you—" I put my arms toward her belly, which isn't showing much yet since she's only a few months along— "look amazing! How are you feeling?"

"So much better," Angela replies with relief. "Morning sickness was horrible throughout the first trimester, but I haven't had it since starting the second."

"That's good," I say, knowing how hard she had it for a while. She has texted us regularly to let us know how she's feeling, and she had felt sick nearly every day for a while.

"Let me show you our room!" Angela points to the staircase leading upstairs. "We're in the Mermaid Room."

"Ooh!" I pick up my suitcase and follow her up the stairs. When I had looked at the website, I saw that all of the guest rooms here are themed. The Mermaid Room is one of my favorites.

Angela leads me to our room and unlocks the door. "Welcome to our abode," she says, opening the door and outstretching her arm to let me enter first.

I walk into the room decked out in seaside and mermaid decor. It's not cheesy or child-like at all. The colors are muted blues, purples, and grays, and it feels cozy and magical. There's only one bed, which we expected, but it's a large king-size, giving Angela and me plenty of space to sleep. We've been friends for so long, this won't be the first time we've shared a bed.

"This looks amazing," I say, setting my suitcase down and taking it all in.

Angela shuts the door behind her. "Michelle and Penny are in the Celestial Room. You'll have to see it later. They have a view of the ocean."

I look out our window, which faces the front of the house. "Lucky bitches," I say with a laugh, and Angela laughs, too.

"Speaking of those lucky bitches, let's go back downstairs and meet them on the porch," Angela suggests. "They have a bottle of wine that I'm sure you'll love."

We head back downstairs, and I follow Angela out to the back deck.

"Summer!" Both Michelle and Penny raise their wine glasses to greet me as we join them. They stand, and I give each of them a hug before we all settle down on the Adirondack chairs situated in a horseshoe shape so we can all see the beach and each other.

"How was your drive?" Penny asks as she pours me a glass of wine.

"It was good, just long," I reply with a laugh. "This place seems amazing, though. Definitely worth the drive."

Penny stands to hand me the glass of white wine, then sits again. "I love it so far, too. I'm glad Michelle found this place online."

I take a sip of my wine. It's a delicious, sweet Riesling.

"So am I," Michelle says. "I was disappointed when the hotels were all sold out, but this place showed up in my search and still had two rooms available. We may have to share beds, but I knew we'd all be okay with that."

"It's totally fine," Angela says before taking a quick sip from her water bottle. "I'm glad they still had availability. I guess this Seaside Festival draws a lot of tourists every year."

"I'm excited for the book signing tomorrow," Penny says.

"Me, too," I reply. "Some of my favorite authors will be there, and I can't wait to have them sign my books."

"Girl, I brought a ton of books with me. I also brought a small cart to haul them around in," Michelle tells us. "I have a list of authors I want to meet!"

"Same," I say, taking another sip of wine.

"Me, too," Penny says.

"Me, three," Angela pipes in, and we all laugh.

We enjoy the sunshine, as well as each other's company, as the ocean breeze tickles our senses. We enjoy the bottle of wine, too, and the three of us polish off a second before we decide to head into town for dinner. Angela drives us in my car, being our designated driver for the weekend.

It feels good being with my friends again. Sure, I have friends back home in Port Townsend—some I've known my whole life, and a few I've met since moving back after college—but my relationship with Michelle, Penny, and Angela is different. We spent our formative young adult lives together and faced several hardships, helping each other through each one we endured. We also share a lot of fun memories. These girls are my rock, like my second group of sisters. This weekend is just what my soul needs.

Summer

Chapter 2

"Good morning," Penny says as Angela and I walk into the dining room.

"Good morning," Angela and I both say as we sit at the table across from Penny and Michelle.

"Did you sleep well last night?" Michelle asks.

I nod. "I did. The bed was really comfy. How about you?"

"I wish I had a bed that comfy at home," Michelle says with a laugh. "I slept really well."

"I agree," Penny says.

"Me, too," Angela adds. "I'm glad we stayed here."

Suddenly, a blond woman in a purple caftan dress emerges from the kitchen, carrying a tray with coffee mugs and a carafe on top. She walks right over to us. "Here's your coffee," she says as she sets everything out in front of us.

"We ordered coffee for all of us," Michelle tells Angela and me.

"Thank you."

"I haven't met you yet," the woman says to me. "You must be Summer."

Although I'm surprised she knows my name, I figure this must be the owner of the inn. My friends probably mentioned my name when they arrived yesterday and told her I would be arriving later. I smile kindly at her and reply, "Yes, that's me."

"It's nice to meet you, Summer." She extends her hand for me to shake. Lorelei wraps her other hand over mine in a warm gesture. "I'm Lorelei, and I own the Sandy Shore Inn. I'm sure glad to have you all staying with us."

"It's nice to meet you," I say before our handshake ends.

"Breakfast is almost ready, and I'll bring it right out for you," she says to all of us. "Today, we're having scrambled eggs, bacon, sausage links, toast, cantaloupe, and a variety of muffins to choose from."

"Sounds delicious." Penny reads my mind.

Lorelei turns and walks back toward the kitchen, and the four of us go about fixing our mugs of coffee. I add a teaspoon of sugar and cream, stirring it in until it's a nice caramel color. As I take my first sip, I notice another B&B guest walk into the dining room. She sits at a small table by herself, and she looks... *sad*. She's absolutely gorgeous, and I wonder what she's doing here all alone. The sullen look on her face makes me want to reach out and give her a hug—but that would be weird to do to a stranger. Hopefully, she's okay.

I tend to worry about other people more than I should. My mom has always told me I have a good motherly instinct. Maybe it's because I have three sisters, two of which are younger than me. Caring for others is something I naturally tend to do, but I've learned it can also be detrimental. After my last relationship ended over a year ago, I realized I can't pour from an empty cup. I need to take care of myself, too. So, although I have the tendency to want to help others—and I still do when I can—I also know I have to make sure my own needs are met.

Sometimes I learn things the hard way. I don't have the best track record in the relationship department. That's why I'm thirty and still single.

Maybe that's why this beautiful blonde sitting alone is sad. Some asshole probably broke her heart.

I need to pull myself from this mental rabbit hole of sadness I'm going down and get back to the exciting day my friends and I have planned. It's not as if I can just walk over to this woman I've never met before and try to make her feel better. If someone did that to me, I'd probably tell them to fuck off and mind their own business.

I turn my attention back to my friends and ask, "Which authors are you most looking forward to meeting today?" As librarians and reading enthusiasts, I'm sure we all have a long list of booths we want to visit.

"All of them," Angela says with a laugh. "But, seriously, I've been dying to meet Charlotte Ann. I adored her last book."

"I haven't read that one yet," Michelle says, "but I enjoyed the others I've read by her."

"I want to meet Maddie Cooper," Penny replies.

Angela nods her head. "Yes! She's on my list, too!"

"How about... everyone?" We all laugh at my joke, although I'm only half-joking. I truly would love to meet every single author at the signing today.

"Ooh!" Michelle says as if she has suddenly remembered something. "What about Mr. Stone Ryder?" She waggles her eyebrows, and we all laugh again.

"Yes, we definitely need to stop by his table," Penny says.

"I wonder if he's as handsome in person as he is in the photos on the back of his books?" Angela asks.

Just then, Lorelei walks back into the room, this time bringing us a basket full of muffins. "Did I hear you mention Stone Ryder's name?" she asks as she sets the basket on the table in front of us.

We all nod, and I explain, "Yes, you did. We're heading to the Seaside Festival's Book Signing today."

Lorelei places her hands on her hips. "Oh, yes. My niece is helping at that event this weekend. She's usually here working with me, but she needed to help her boyfriend with his booth."

"Her boyfriend?" I ask, wondering which author she's talking about.

Lorelei nods, then leans in as if she's going to let us in on a secret. "She's dating the one and only Stone Ryder."

My jaw hits the floor. Did she just say that? Embarrassment washes over me, wondering if she overheard us talking about how handsome we think he is.

"Your niece is dating Stone Ryder?" Angela asks, sounding equally stunned.

Lorelei smiles. "She sure is. Met him when he came to town for the book signing last year. He stayed right here at the inn. Since then, he's bought his own home in Seaside that he stays at when he's here... which is practically year-round now."

"Wow! That's so cool," Michelle says, still clearly as

surprised as the rest of us. "I read an article about him buying a second home in Seaside, but I had forgotten about it until now."

"I can't believe he's dating your niece!" Penny's eyes practically bulge from their sockets. "He's like a celebrity!"

Lorelei nods. "Yes, but he hasn't let the fame go to his head. He's one of the kindest people you'll ever meet, which I suppose you'll discover today."

"We'll be sure to say hi to your niece for you if we see her," Michelle says.

"Oh, please do!" Lorelei winks at us, then turns and walks back to the kitchen.

The four of us look at each other in shock before Angela says, "Wow, that's pretty cool."

"I can't believe it! What are the odds?" I say, still surprised that *the* Stone Ryder stayed here a year ago, met Lorelei's niece, and is now in a relationship with her.

"Maybe if we tell Stone and her niece that Lorelei says hi, we'll get the VIP treatment," Penny says.

"We already have the VIP package for this event," Michelle reminds her. "But

maybe we'll get a little extra attention for name-dropping and mentioning we're staying at the Sandy Shore Inn." She waggles her eyebrows, and we all laugh. I know my friends are joking, but it still feels cool to have some sort of connection to the famous author.

After we finish breakfast and get up to leave, I notice the blond woman sitting alone is softly crying to herself. I wish I could do something to make her feel better, but I don't know what to do. Hopefully, she'll be all right. Lorelei is a kind woman who seems rather empathic and wise—maybe she'll be able to offer her good advice. As we leave the dining room, I silently wish her well and hope I'll see her again during our stay here—hopefully happier than she is now.

I offer to drive the four of us into town for the book signing. It's being held at the Seaside Hotel, which is one of the larger hotels in town located right on the beach. After I park in the garage, we make our way inside and find the ballroom where the event is taking place. We each present our tickets, and the lady hands us our VIP bags filled with goodies. I can't wait to rummage through it to see what we got, but there's no time for that now. We have authors to meet and books to have signed! We all look at the map showing where each author's table is located.

"I guess we can just start at one end and work our way through," Angela suggests.

"Sounds like a plan. Let's get started!" With her cart in tow, Michelle leads the way, and we begin our day full of books and authors.

* * *

"This has been an amazing day!" Penny plops into one of the chairs and sets a couple of books on the table in front of her.

"Yeah, it has," I agree as I sit across from her, also setting down three new books I purchased from authors.

The four of us make ourselves comfortable at the table, sitting for the first time since arriving at the book signing two hours ago. We've made it through the entire thing, meeting almost every single author with a booth here, including all the ones we wanted to make a point to meet. Michelle's cart is full, not only with books for herself, but she has been kind enough to carry some of ours as well. We still all end up with a few books in our hands to carry, too.

"I can't believe we got Stone Ryder's autograph!" Angela says, holding up her signed copy of his famous novel *Fire and Ice*.

"Neither can I," Michelle says.

"Both he and Olivia were so nice," I add. "When we mentioned we were staying at the Sandy Shore Inn, they lit up and seemed so grateful for supporting her aunt's business."

"Yeah, they were really nice," Penny says.

"All the authors were nice," Michelle adds. "And I met a few new-to-me authors I can't wait to read, like Monica Misho-Grems."

"Yes! I bought her *Secrets of the Arlington* book. It sounds so good," Angela says.

"I did, too." I hold up the book that happens to be in my pile on the table in front of me.

"Amanda Shelley was a sweetheart," Michelle says. "Oh, and KA Graham!"

"Yes!" Penny agrees. "I also bought a book from each of them."

I rummage through the VIP bag, looking at the books I put in there. I bought so many today, I can't remember what I got. "Yeah, I bought *Resilience* by Amanda Shelley, and *Madness* by KA Graham and Barb Shuler. I guess they co-write a lot together."

I continue looking through my bag to see what kinds of goodies are included in it. I pull out a few bookmarks to see who they're from. Denise Wells, M. Leigh Morhaime, and one from a local bookstore called Booked at the Beach.

Huh... that's a cute name for a bookstore. Maybe we'll have to stop by there later. I'm a sucker for bookstores, especially smaller, local shops with clever names.

"Hey, guys, we should check this place out," I say to my friends, holding up the bookmark for them to see.

Michelle squints from across the table. "What is it?"

"Booked at the Beach," I reply. "It's a bookstore in town."

"Cute name. I'm game," Penny says.

"Me, too. You know I can't resist a trip to a bookstore." Angela smiles.

"Cool. Let's stop there before we go back to the B&B," Michelle says.

We stay at the book signing a little while longer, then decide to leave. Since we bought the VIP package, we get to come back tonight for the VIP dinner, but that's not for several hours. We have plenty of time to go back to the Sandy Shore Inn and change into our dressier clothes for the dinner. I'm excited for tonight. Most, if not all, of the authors will be at the dinner, and there will be opportunities to interact with them. We may even luck out and have one seated at our table.

After loading my car with our bags—and cart—full of books, I type the address to Booked at the Beach into my GPS. It's a short drive, and luckily, there's a parking spot open on the street right in front of the store. I parallel park, then cut the engine.

"What a cute place," Michelle says from the backseat.

I look at the older, ornate building the store is located in. There are several books on display in the shop's window, along with fairy lights all around them. It looks very inviting.

"Let's go in," Angela says as she opens the front passenger side door.

We all exit the car and walk toward the store's entrance. Penny opens the door and holds it open for all of us to walk in. As soon as I do, I adore Booked at the Beach. Billie Holiday's voice softly sings over the shop's speakers, and the rows of bookshelves are inviting. Even the vanilla scent in the air makes the atmosphere seem warm.

"Welcome in," a deep voice says to my right. I turn and see the man who greeted us standing behind the checkout counter.

And he's handsome. Like, drop-dead hot as hell, handsome.

My belly muscles clench.

Damn. I haven't felt those muscles in a while.

"Thanks," Angela replies for all of us.

The guy smiles at me, turning his hotness up about ten notches. I quickly smile in

return, then look away and walk in the opposite direction. Jesus, what was that all about? A good-looking guy smiles at me, and I practically run for the hills? I know it's been awhile since I've caught the attention of someone as handsome as this guy, but I don't need to act like a freakin' leper. What's wrong with me?

I look up at the genres listed at the top of the bookshelves. I chuckle to myself as I realize I'm in the self-help section. *Of course, I am.* Perfect.

I walk around the corner. Religion. I walk to the next aisle. Travel. *Where's the damn fiction section*? As I look around, I realize I must be on the nonfiction side of the store. I find my friends on the other side, closer to the hot guy behind the counter, all looking at the fiction books. Did I really get so flustered from that guy smiling at me that I wandered too far away from where I wanted to be?

What a fucking metaphor for my life.

Taking a deep breath, I try to shake off this scattered feeling I have. How can I let a guy make me feel this way, simply from smiling in my direction? This is dumb.

I join Penny in the suspense section and peruse the books. I've already spent a lot of money at the book signing today, so I'm not sure I'll buy anything else. I'm just intrigued to visit this store and look around.

"Can I help you find anything?" The hairs on the back of my neck stand at attention, and goosebumps cover my arms at the sound of his voice.

I turn around and see the sexy man from behind the counter now standing just inches away from me.

"Oh, I'm just looking," I stammer, unable to stop admiring this man's blue eyes, short brown hair that's a little messy on top, and five o'clock shadow covering the lower half of his gorgeous face.

"If you're looking for a good book to read, I highly recommend this one." He pulls a book off the shelf and holds it out toward me.

I recognize it immediately. "Ah, yes. Stone Ryder's newest release," I say, suddenly feeling a little more normal since we're talking about books.

"Have you read it?" he asks. "He's actually a Seaside local now."

"So I've heard," I say with a chuckle. "And, yes, I read the book last week. I actually had him sign my copy today."

His eyebrows shoot up in surprise. "Wow! So, you went to the Seaside Festival's Book Signing?"

Nodding, I reply, "Yeah. My friends and I came to town specifically for that."

He places the book back on the shelf. "Ah, so you're book connoisseurs?" He smiles, and I get the feeling he's—*dare I say it*—flirting with me.

The realization brings back the nerves I so quickly shook off just seconds ago. So much for feeling calm.

"Y-yeah. We're all librarians, so..."

"Oh! That's cool. A librarian—" he points at me, then points back at himself— "bookstore worker... we have very similar jobs."

I smile, then turn to look at Angela behind me, but I notice she's not there anymore. Where did she go?

"So, did you meet a lot of great authors today?" hottie bookstore guy asks, pulling my attention back to him.

"Oh, um..." I'm so flustered; this is ridiculous. "Yeah, we did. We get to go back for the VIP dinner tonight, too."

"Do you? Well, what a coincidence... I'll be there, too."

This time, my eyebrows fly up in surprise. He's going to the VIP dinner tonight? I'll get to see this beautiful man again?

"Wow, that's... cool," I say, unsure of what else to say at this moment. Idly, I wonder where all my friends went. It feels as if Mr. Sexy here and I are the only two people in the shop.

"Yeah, it is," he says, shoving his hands in his jeans pockets, keeping eye contact with me a bit longer than what's socially acceptable—unless you're flirting. "Well, I should let you get back to shopping. Let me know if you have any questions."

I nod and smile. "Thanks. I will."

He turns and walks away, and I can't help but wonder if I'll see him at the dinner tonight.

Garrick

Chapter 3

"Hey, Sophie. Do you still have that extra ticket for the book signing's VIP dinner thing tonight?"

Sophie turns her head and peers at me over the top of her reading glasses.

"Yeah, but why?"

Shrugging a shoulder, I try to play it cool. I can't tell her it's because this hot girl came into the shop today, she's going to be there tonight, and I want the chance to see her again. "I guess out of curiosity. I mean, it's not like I have anything else to do tonight."

"Really?" She squints as if she doesn't quite believe me.

I chuckle. "Yes, really. Can I be your date?"

"Ew, gross." Sophie rolls her eyes and turns back toward her computer. "I don't go on dates with my brother."

I laugh. "Not *literally* your date. Jesus."

"You know you're supposed to dress up for this dinner, right?"

"What, like formal? Black tie?" I ask, second guessing my idea to go. I'm more of a casual guy. I don't even own a suit.

"No, no. Nothing like that," she says. "You could wear jeans or khakis with a nice button-up shirt. It's not formal, just nice."

"Okay. I can do that," I reply, mentally picking out what I could wear.

"We'll close the shop an hour early at five o'clock and go home to change before going. Sound good?"

"Sounds like a plan," I reply, although now I feel a little guilty. "Sorry you have to close the shop early, though. I can stay and keep it open like we originally planned."

Sophie looks at me and shakes her head. "No, no. It's only an hour early, and I'm sure it won't make a difference. Most book lovers in town will probably be at the dinner anyway. Besides, I originally asked if you wanted to go to the dinner with me, so it's no problem."

"Okay, if you say so, boss," I say with a shrug.

"That's right, I am your boss. Don't forget it." Sophie pokes my arm with her finger and chuckles.

"Yeah... my bossy little sister." I shake my head and poke her in her arm in return.

She gasps. "Hey, now, watch yourself, or you'll get fired."

I walk out of the back office with my hands up. "Ooh, I'm scared!"

As I walk out to the store, I see Sophie giving me the finger from the corner of my eye.

I love my sister.

The last couple of hours of work seem to go by slowly. A few customers come in, but it's pretty slow. All I can think about is what to wear tonight and what I'm going to say when I see the beautiful woman I met earlier today. I don't even know her name. That'll have to be the first thing I ask her when I see her tonight.

This isn't like me. I don't go after every pretty girl who comes into the bookstore, or anywhere else I happen to be. I just couldn't help myself. There was something about this girl that attracted me to her. I haven't gone on a date in nearly a year. No one has caught my eye like this in a long time. The only downside is that she mentioned that she and her friends are in town for the book signing, so that means she's not a local. I don't know where she lives, but that could obviously prove to be an issue. Tonight could very well be the last time I ever see this woman. Maybe that's why I feel an urgency to see her again.

After Sophie and I close the shop, she drives us home to get ready. We don't have a lot of time—not that I need a lot of time to get ready. But we're out the door and back in her car on our way to the event in practically no time flat. I offered to drive, but she insisted on doing it herself, which is usually par for the course with Sophie. She likes to be in charge; hence, why she opened her own bookstore practically straight out of college instead of working for someone else. Her business has done well for the past three years, though, so hats off to her.

When we arrive at the Seaside Hotel, we make our way through the lobby to the ballroom where this event is being held. I have no idea what to expect when we walk through those doors, but this isn't the first time I've attended something last minute and wasn't sure of what to expect. There was that time in India when I somehow ended up at a wedding. Now *that* was a party! Or, the time I got a wild hair and decided on a whim to fly to Rio so I could experience

Carnival. That was quite a party, too. I've had the chance to experience a lot of interesting things most people I know haven't, and I'm grateful. Now, while I'm sure this VIP author dinner shindig is going to be a good time, I have a feeling it's not going to be as wild as some other things I've done.

However, I may be a little intimidated when I see *her*.

We find the ballroom and join the short line waiting to get in. They're checking everyone's tickets. Sophie opens her purse and pulls out two paper slips, handing one of them to me. "Here's yours," she says.

"Thanks," I say as I read the print. *The Seaside Festival Book Signing VIP Author Dinner* is scrolled in the middle with a border of books around it. This will definitely be a first for me.

We move forward in line and present our tickets to the lady checking them. She marks something on them with a pen, then smiles and lets us into the ballroom. I have to say, I'm a little underwhelmed with the place as we walk in. Sure, the tables are decorated with crisp, white tablecloths and pretty centerpieces of books adorned with fairy lights, but nothing too fancy. It kind of reminds me of our window display at the shop.

"We're at table nine," Sophie says, pointing at the number at the bottom of our tickets.

"Cool. Let's find numero nueve," I reply, hoping I see the girl I came here for soon.

It doesn't take long for us to find our table, and I almost jump for joy when I see the blond-haired beauty already seated at our table, next to an empty chair. Could this be kismet? I think it's definitely something.

"Hello again," I say as we walk up to our table.

"Again?" Sophie says, obviously confused.

The four women at the table look up at us, all with surprised looks on their faces.

The one with dark, wavy hair speaks up first. "Oh, hi! You work at the bookstore, right?"

I nod. "Yes." I point to Sophie, next to me. "This is my sister Sophie, the owner of the shop." I want to make it clear right away that she's not my date.

"Oh, how nice! We loved your shop," the same woman says as Sophie and I take our seats.

"Thank you so much," Sophie replies. "I must've been in the back office when you came in."

"I'm Michelle, by the way."

"I'm Angela," the woman sitting next to Michelle says.

"I'm Penny," the next one says.

I look to the blonde sitting to my right. "I'm Summer." She smiles, and I can't help but smile back at her. We hold each other's eye contact before she asks, "And what's your name?"

I chuckle, realizing I had introduced Sophie but not myself. "I'm Garrick," I say and force myself to break eye contact with her and look at the rest of the table as well.

"What are the chances you're seated at the same table as us?" Penny quips, and I notice the subtle look she gives Summer, raising her eyebrows slightly.

"Yeah, quite the coincidence," I agree, and I look at Summer, too.

Summer turns her head toward me again and smiles.

Suddenly, a server arrives at our table and places dinner salads in front of each of us. We thank her, then she asks

Sophie and me what we'd like to drink. We each order a glass
of red wine, and then she walks away. I notice our four new
friends already have a glass of wine, except for Angela, who
just has water.

The six of us talk as we eat our salads. I learn that the four
of them have been friends since their days at Pacific Northwest University, and they get together at least once a year.
They all live in Washington, although not all in the same city.
Summer lives the furthest away, all the way up in Port
Townsend. This news bums me out a little. I was hoping she
lived somewhere closer to Seaside, or at least Portland, but
that's not the case. I've never been to Port Townsend, but
I've heard about it and thought about visiting before...
maybe now I'll have a reason to do so.

We finish our salads, and our server comes to replace our
salad plates with our main course meals. I have baked chicken
placed in front of me, while Sophie and a couple others have
steak, and Summer has salmon. We all have mashed potatoes
and green beans accompanying our main dish.

Sophie leans over and says, "Sorry, I ordered chicken for
my plus-one. I wasn't sure who I was going to bring when I
RSVP'd, or if anyone would even end up coming with me.
Lucky you."

"No worries," I reply. Chicken is fine, although the
salmon on Summer's plate looks delicious. "And thanks
again for bringing me."

Sophie leans in a little closer and whispers, "Uh-huh... I
think I know why you wanted to come now."

I look at Sophie and grin. She rolls her eyes, then goes
about cutting her steak. I suppose it wouldn't take a genius
to figure out why I asked to come last minute, considering I

met these ladies this afternoon and have been giving my attention to Summer all evening.

"Sophie, how long have you owned Booked at the Beach?" Michelle asks.

"Three years now," she says.

"Wow, that's awesome," Michelle replies. "What made you decide to open a book store?"

Sophie takes a sip of her wine, then replies, "Reading has always been a passion of mine, but I studied business in college. After I graduated with my degree, I started working for a company and quickly hated it." She chuckles. "I felt like I was on a bad episode of *The Office* every day when I went to work—like I was the only person who felt things were so utterly ridiculous, it was funny, but really *not* funny at all."

"Oh, that must've been awful," Summer says, grimacing.

"It was." Sophie chuckles again before continuing, "After our grandfather passed away, I decided to move to Seaside. The bookstore was for sale, and I decided to buy it and put my degree to work as a business owner. It was the best decision I could've made."

"That's amazing. Good for you!" Michelle says.

"Thanks. I have to admit I'm pretty proud of myself for being a successful female business owner under the age of thirty."

"That *is* amazing," Summer says before turning her attention to me. "And how long have you worked at Booked at the Beach?"

I finish chewing the bite of chicken in my mouth, then reply, "Only a couple of months now. But I'm not an official employee. I'm just helping my sister during this busy time of year while I'm still in town."

Summer stops chewing for a moment and looks at me as if she's trying to figure me out, which makes sense. After all, why wouldn't a guy my age have a real job? I feel the need to explain a little more.

"I'm a freelance writer," I say, and Summer's eyes soften a little. "I've spent the past couple of years traveling around the world, writing articles for various media outlets. I love exploring, and I love writing, so I've been living the dream."

Summer's eyes widen. "That's amazing," she says, her lips curving up in a smile. She is so beautiful, and I can't help but smile back at her. "Thanks. I feel

blessed to be able to do what I do."

"Where have you traveled to?" Penny asks, and I force myself to break eye contact with Summer to look at her friend.

"All over," I reply with a short laugh. "I've been to all the continents, minus Antarctica. I haven't found a reason to go there yet."

"Wow! Seriously, that's so cool," Angela says. "Where was the last place you went?"

"I was in South America," I begin to explain. "In February, I flew to Rio for Carnival—which was *amazing,* by the way. I stayed there for a couple of weeks, then decided to fly up to French Guiana for a week before heading to Caracas, Venezuela for another week. Then, I flew back home to Portland to recover for a few days before I came here to stay in Seaside for a few months."

I look at Summer, whose mouth is slack, seemingly surprised by what I've said again. "So, you just spent a month traveling? In South America?" she asks. "That sounds amazing."

I nod. "It was. Like I said, I feel blessed."

Summer nods, then looks back at her food and takes another bite of her delicious-looking salmon. I watch as her lips close around her fork, and I realize I'm actually jealous of a piece of silverware. I didn't think that was possible.

"That is *so* cool," Michelle says, and I turn toward her, pulling my attention away from Summer's luscious lips. "Where can I find some of your published articles?"

"I've written for several travel magazines and websites. You can find some of my articles in *Global Traveler, Travel and Leisure,* and *Wanderlust,*" I say, looking back at Summer just as the word *lust* comes out of my mouth.

I hold her gaze, admiring her blueish-green eyes. They remind me of the ocean, and I want to dive in and learn more about Summer. She's learned a little about my life tonight, but I feel as if I've only learned a small fraction of hers. I want to know more about this beautiful woman, and I pray I'll get the chance to do so.

I slowly smile, and Summer blushes. Then, suddenly, there's an announcement over the PA system in the ballroom.

"Welcome, everyone!" We all turn toward the stage to see the woman at the mic. "It's so wonderful to see so many fellow book lovers here at the fifth annual Seaside Festival's Book Signing VIP Dinner Extravaganza!" Everyone erupts in cheers, including my sister and all of the women seated around me at our table. Once the crowd dies down, the woman on stage continues, "Authors will start mingling soon, so feel free to get up, walk around, and talk with your favorites. Photo ops will also be available, and dessert will be served following all of that. So, everyone, please enjoy the rest of your dinner and each other's company!"

Everyone claps again as the woman sets the mic back in the stand and exits the stage. I still have no idea what to expect after dinner. Authors will be mingling? So, everyone can just walk around and talk to authors and take pictures? I have no idea if I'll have the chance to talk with Summer again once we get up from this table, so I need to take my shot at asking what she's doing later.

I wipe my mouth with my napkin, then set it on top of my nearly empty plate. "What are your plans after this?" I lean over and ask her.

"Oh, um..." Summer looks at me, seeming nervous all of a sudden. "I don't know, actually. Why?"

Smiling, I ask, "Would you like to meet for drinks? The hotel bar here is actually one of the best in town."

She smiles in return, her eyes sparkling. "That sounds fun. I'd like that." Then, as if she's suddenly remembering something, her smile fades. "I rode here with my friends, though."

"That's okay. I rode here with my sister."

"What about me?" Sophie says, leaning in closer.

I chuckle. "I was just saying I rode here with you." *Maybe plan B will work.* "Summer and I were just saying it would be fun to hang out after this VIP thing is over. Want to go to the bar for an after party?"

Sophie clicks her tongue, giving me a *I know what you're doing* look. "Sure," she finally says. "That sounds fun."

I smile at my sister, then turn back to Summer, who asks her friends the same thing. They all agree that going to the hotel bar sounds like a good idea once this shindig is over.

Thank God. I get to spend more time with Summer tonight, even if it is in a group setting along with my sister and her friends. There's something intriguing about Summer that makes me want to get to know her better. It's not just the physical attraction I feel toward her anymore; it's a strange feeling of kismet that I can't explain. All I know is that I can't let this opportunity pass me by. And I *cannot* wait for this VIP dinner to finally be over.

Summer

Chapter 4

My head sinks into the plush pillow. The soft, silkiness of the fabric feels good against my cheek. This bed is beyond comfy, and I don't want to wake up. I slept extremely well after an incredible night out, and I want to savor this feeling of contentment.

My eyes flutter open as the mattress jostles, reminding me I'm not alone. Before this weekend, I hadn't slept with another person in so long, I'd gotten used to waking up alone every day.

"Good morning," Angela says.

"Good morning," I reply.

She sits up, stretching her arms over her head. "I wish I didn't have to leave today," she says as she yawns.

Keeping my head on my soft pillow, I reply, "I wish you didn't either."

Angela stands and turns around to face me. "You're lucky you're staying an extra day. When are you heading back home, anyway?"

"I'm going to my sister's house tomorrow and staying until next Saturday."

"That'll be a nice little vacay for you," Angela says before scooting off toward the bathroom.

"For sure," I say, pulling the covers up to my chin and relaxing once again.

This has already been *more* than a nice little vacay for me. Spending time with my friends in Seaside has been wonderful. Going to the book signing and getting to see some of my favorite authors was incredible. Meeting Garrick and spending time with him at dinner last night, then again at the bar afterward, was completely unexpected.

The more I get to know him, the more I like him. Sure, he's good looking and charming, but I'm also captivated by his life experiences. I've never met anyone who travels the world and gets paid to write about it. Honestly, I'm intrigued by his lifestyle. I don't know how much he gets paid for the articles he writes, but it must be enough to get by. I'm guessing he doesn't just come to Seaside to help his sister at her shop, but to also make extra money between his trips. I don't know for sure, but it's a plausible explanation for how he's able to live the way he does.

Before the girls and I left the bar last night, Garrick asked if he could see me again before I leave town. Of course, I said yes. We'd been flirting with each other all evening, so I was glad he asked, and I was also grateful I made the decision to stay another night in Seaside by myself. When I planned this trip, I figured it would be nice to stay an extra night at the beach alone. I could relax, read a book, basically do whatever I want before spending the rest of the week in Portland with my sisters. But now, I have a date with the sexy bookstore-working, freelance-writing, world traveler, and I cannot wait to see where this evening takes us.

I hear the water turn on in the bathroom. Angela must've decided to take a shower. I look at the alarm clock on the bedside table and see that it's barely eight o'clock. I got plenty of sleep, but it feels good to laze around in bed a while longer. After all, it's not like I have anywhere to be. We're meeting for breakfast downstairs at nine thirty before the three of them leave. Then, I'll have the entire afternoon to myself before I meet Garrick for dinner tonight.

My phone buzzes, notifying me of a text. I reach over to grab my phone from the side table. I expect it to be Michelle or Penny, but I'm pleasantly surprised to find a text from Garrick.

We had exchanged numbers before we left the bar last night. He said he would text me if he was running late for our date for some reason, or I could do the same if I end up running late. I didn't think he'd message me so early in the morning.

I swipe my phone screen to unlock it and read his message.

> Good morning, Summer! I had a great time last night. I just wanted to say I'm glad we met, and I'm looking forward to getting together again later. Can't wait!

His text makes me smile. What a sweet gesture. It's a good feeling to know he's looking forward to seeing me, just as I'm looking forward to seeing him. I type out a quick reply and hit send.

Good morning! I had fun last night, too.
I'll see you at 6:00 tonight. Can't wait!

After Angela and I are both showered, dressed, and ready for the day, we go downstairs to the dining room to meet Michelle and Penny. They're already sitting at a table when we walk in.

"Good morning," we all say to one another as Angela and I sit.

"I'm so bummed we're leaving today," Angela says. "I wish we could stay longer, like Summer."

"Mmhmm," Michelle replies. "I'm sure Summer is glad she decided to stay an extra night." She winks at me. "I hope you have fun on your date tonight."

My smile widens. "Thank you. I hope I do, too."

"He texted her this morning," Angela informs our friends.

"Oh, really?" Penny leans closer, resting her elbow on the table. "What did he say?"

Although I'm excited, I want to play it off like it's not that big of a deal. "He just said he's excited to see me later."

"Ooh!" Michelle gives me a sly smile. "Garrick was so into you last night. Do you think anything will come of this?"

I shrug just as Penny says something under her breath that only Michelle heard, and they both giggle.

"What?" I ask, wondering what was so funny.

Penny shakes her head, leans closer, and whispers, "I said hopefully Summer will come."

I burst into laughter, along with Angela. Michelle and Penny continue to snicker as well.

"Oh, my God," I say as I calm back down. "That's funny."

"Well... when was the last time you..."

"Had sex?" I complete Michelle's question for her.

She nods, and I shake my head.

"It's been awhile. More than a year ago," I say before leaning in and whispering, "But I can take care of things myself."

Penny gives me a high five. "That's right, girlfriend," she says right before Lorelei appears at our table with a basket full of muffins.

"Good morning, ladies," she says, setting the basket on our table. "Can I get you all coffee?"

"Yes, please," each of us replies.

"I hope you've all enjoyed your stay," she says.

"We have, for sure. This place is beautiful," Penny tells her, and we all agree.

"I'm glad you liked it." Lorelei looks at me. "And lucky you, you get to stay another night!"

I nod. "I'm glad I chose to stay. I plan to sit on the back deck and watch the ocean waves as I read one of the new books I bought yesterday."

"That sounds delightful," Lorelei says in a sing-song voice. "If you have time, you should stop in the shop for a Tarot reading, too." She winks at me, then trots off to the kitchen again.

"Have you ever had a Tarot reading before?" Angela asks.

I shake my head. "No. Have you?"

"No, but it sounds interesting."

"I had a reading once," Michelle says. "It was definitely

interesting. She predicted that I was going to get married within the next year, and Cooper proposed a month later."

"Wow, that's pretty amazing," I reply. "I've never considered getting a Tarot reading before, but it does sound like it could be fascinating."

"You should do it," Penny says. "It might be fun."

Lorelei returns with our coffee, and I ask when a good time to get a reading would be. She tells me to come see her at one o'clock.

Now I have two dates today.

We enjoy our breakfast, and after we're done, I help my friends load Michelle's car with their luggage. We all agree to get together again sooner than later and give hugs all around before they get in the car and drive away, leaving me all to myself.

Don't get me wrong, I love spending time with my friends, and I already miss them, but I also enjoy having time to myself. I turn on my heel, head back into the B&B to retrieve my book in my room, then go out to the back deck and find an Adirondack chair with a good view of the Pacific.

Before I know it, I'm several chapters into *Resilience* by Amanda Shelley, thoroughly enjoying the story, as well as the sound of the waves in the near distance. The alarm I set on my phone is going off, alerting me that it's time for my Tarot reading with Lorelei. I go inside, into the gift shop by the front entrance. The shop is full of candles, crystals, and all sorts of New Age stuff. There's a wall full of Tarot decks for sale, and another wall boasting several artfully designed Ouija boards. It's quite an interesting shop, and I'm instantly drawn to the magic of it all.

"Summer! You're here!" I hear Lorelei's voice before I see her. I turn around and

see her standing just a few feet away. "I do readings over here. Come, sit!"

I walk over to where she is and sit in the red high-back chair she tells me to sit in. She sits across from me, on the other side of a small, round table. "Go ahead and pick up the deck," she says, pointing at the deck of Tarot cards on the table. "Shuffle the cards, all the while thinking about the things you'd like the cards to tell you."

I nod and do as she says, but I'm not sure what to think about. I'd like to know everything. Will I be financially secure? Will I meet the man of my dreams? Will I ever get married or have kids? Will I always live in my hometown, Port Townsend?

I can't concentrate on one topic, so I let my mind wander to all of the things I want to know. Hopefully, that's okay. I don't know how this Tarot card stuff works.

I finish shuffling the cards, then set them back on the table in front of me. Lorelei spreads the cards into a fan shape. "Pick three and lay them on the table, face up," she tells me, and, again, I do as she says.

Lorelei examines the cards, and I wonder what they mean. One has a guy with what looks like a shovel next to a bush full of yellow orbs, another has a guy who appears to be upside down, and the third one shows a woman pouring water from pitchers with several bright stars above her in the sky.

She points to the first one, her long purple fingernail tapping the man with the shovel. "This card represents your past. It's the Seven of Pentacles." Looking closer at the card now, I notice the yellow orbs in the picture have stars inside them. "This card tells me that things you cultivated grew very well for you. Like the man in the picture, you enjoyed the fruits of your labor, and you're thankful for all you've achieved in life."

Well, so far, she's on track. I always worked hard in school, which caused me to graduate with honors, which ultimately helped me land my first job as a librarian at Port Townsend's public library. I've had a successful career working there for the past seven years and love it.

Lorelei continues, "Like all sevens, the Seven of Pentacles represents creativity. The card's position, representing the past, means you have an important influence from your past. You can't change the past, but you can learn from it by acknowledging what you've been through and under-standing it better; thus, not repeating the same mistakes you've made." Lorelei pauses and closes her eyes. Her finger-nail lightly taps the card three times, and then she opens her eyes and looks at me. "I'm sensing you've been very successful in your career, but it's your social life where there may have been mistakes made. Perhaps relationships that didn't work out. You tend to forge relationships with partners who all have the same flaws. Think about what those past partners weren't giving you and learn from that." She pauses again, then asks, "Can I see your hand, Summer? I'd like to read your palm."

Her request takes me by surprise. "Sh-sure," I stammer, outstretching my arm with my palm facing up. She takes my hand in both of hers, examining it closely, running her finger over some of the lines.

Her eyes look back up at me. "You've met someone

recently. This person is going to play an important role in your life. He's not like those in your past." She gives my hand a light squeeze and smiles kindly, then lets go of my hand. I pull it back, stunned by what she just said. I *did* just meet someone. Garrick. He's going to play an important role in my life? He's not like my past? She's nailed everything she's said about my past so far, so could she be right about Garrick, too?

Before I have time to dwell on her words, Lorelei continues, "The Seven of Pentacles also reminds you that any long-term plans you made always take time. Don't get frustrated when things take longer to cultivate than you thought they would take. Not everything happens all at once. You may see your friends' plans taking shape sooner than yours, but that's okay. Your life has its own path; things will happen when they're meant to be."

Is she still talking about relationships? Is she referring to my friends all settling down and having babies, while I'm still searching for *the one*?

Lorelei's finger moves to the middle card. She lightly taps it a few times as she appears to be thinking about what to say. She looks at me again and says, "This card represents the present. It's the Hanged Man—but don't let that frighten you. The Hanged Man doesn't mean anything bad. As you can see in the picture, he's not in distress. By hanging upside down like this, he's sacrificing himself to achieve something, which is the message here. This card is a sign that you need to sacrifice—or rather, release something—in your life to move on. Being in the present position means there's something—or someone—in the here and now who will be a pivotal influence on your life. By taking immediate action, you can mold your future and change the potential outcome that could be a result of your past. Keep in mind that it may be difficult, sad, or even painful to sacrifice whatever it is you need to let go of that's hindering your future, but it's necessary. You need to clear the cobwebs of your past to receive what the universe has in store for you. You may procrastinate or try to deny it at first, but the fact is that if you don't sacrifice something, you'll stay stuck where you are... like the Hanged Man here."

She taps the card again, and I look at her, stunned. I feel gutted. I hope my last card can shed some light for me. I'm not sure I like Lorelei right now.

"This last card is The Star, and here it represents your future. This is a good card to have in this position, as it's full of optimism, like a light at the end of the tunnel."

Thank God. At least my future looks bright! My body relaxes, and I realize my shoulders are practically at my ears.

"There's a lot of positive energy coming from this card. The future position means there's a critical element about to come, but to understand it, you must examine the previous cards. Remember, you can't change things that happened in your past, but you can change the course of your future by analyzing your past and taking action in the present. This card also shows that you have an opportunity coming your way. Something that will make your life better in some way. Be open to positive changes coming your way; don't be blind or misled in how you *think* things should go. Trust your gut and have faith in yourself."

Wow. Just wow. Lorelei has hit the nail on the head in regard to my past, and while my present sounds a little unnerving, my future will be good as long as I follow my gut instincts and let go of the things I need to in order to move on. Talk about a reality check. And the fact that a person I recently met is going to play an important role in my life? *Hello?!?* What am I supposed to think of all this information?

"Don't feel scared or discouraged," Lorelei says, as if she can read my mind. "Whoever this new person in your life is, they will be a positive and important person to you. Again, trust your gut and don't be afraid because of your past. Things will not turn out the same. Your future is very bright."

I'm speechless. I look at Lorelei, my mouth hanging open, unsure of what to say.

She smiles, then leans in and whispers, "He's worth it."

My hand flies to my throat as if it's trying to catch my heart that's just leapt there as well. Lorelei winks at me, and I don't understand how she can know the new person in my life is a man, or that he'll be worth it.

"Do—do you mean he'll be worth it in a romantic sense?" I ask, finally finding some words to say.

Lorelei nods. "That's the feeling I have. He's not like the others, and he's not all you'll expect him to be, but that's okay. Always remember to trust your instincts, Summer. You've been good about that in the past, which is why things never worked out with anyone else. But, this time, according to your cards, you may need to sacrifice something in order for things to work. Trust your gut. It will be worth it."

I thank Lorelei and pay her. She asks if she can give me a hug before I leave, and I do. She gives me a warm hug, and it actually calms me. The energy Lorelei exudes is positive, almost motherly. No matter what my cards said, it's hard not to like this woman. I'm glad I met her, and I don't regret getting a Tarot reading today.

I walk back out to the back porch, but instead of reading my book, I decide to take a walk on the beach. I have a lot to think about. Not only that, but I also have my date with Garrick to look forward to later. After all the information Lorelei just divulged, I'm afraid it'll be difficult for me to act natural around him. Hopefully, a walk on the beach will help clear my head and relax again.

Chapter 5

As I walk into the blue building resembling a lighthouse, I try to shake off the nerves I'm feeling. Garrick suggested we meet here at Norma's Seafood and Steak, one of Seaside's best restaurants. I smile immediately when I see him waiting for me in the foyer. He looks handsome as ever in his button-up gray shirt, the short sleeves showing off his muscular biceps. I imagine how warm and secure it would feel to have his arms around me.

I quickly shove those thoughts aside and focus on the here and now.

"Hi, Summer," he says, walking toward me. "You look beautiful."

"Thank you. You look good yourself," I reply, just as a hostess approaches us.

"Two?" she asks, holding two menus.

"Yes," Garrick replies.

"Follow me," the young hostess says, and we follow her to a table. We take our seats, and she places our menus on the table in front of us. "Your server will be with you shortly," she says before walking away.

I look around the restaurant, which honestly looks more like a nice diner than one of the best restaurants in town. Don't get me wrong, it's nice and clean, it's just not what I expected.

"I know it doesn't look like much," Garrick says as if he read my mind, "but the food here is phenomenal. Trust me."

His choice of words—*trust me*—remind me of how Lorelei told me to trust my instincts.

"So, what did you do today?" he asks, pulling me out of my thoughts.

"I had a really nice day," I tell him. "After Michelle, Penny, and Angela left, I sat on the back deck by the beach and read one of the new books I bought."

"That sounds nice," Garrick says.

"It was. A beautiful view and relaxing spot to read."

Our server arrives at our table, and we put in our drink orders. Garrick and I turn our attention back to each other after she walks away.

"I also got a Tarot card reading," I say, wondering what his response will be.

"You did?" He rests his elbows on the table as he leans a bit closer to me. "How did that turn out?"

"It was interesting. I'd never had one before. The way she described my past and present seemed pretty accurate, and my future seemed hopeful, so that's good."

"That's wild. I've had my cards read a couple of times before. Both times, I felt as if they were spot on. Even what they each said about my future turned out to make sense later on."

"Wow, that's amazing," I reply, curious to know what his own readings said, but also not wanting to ask. If I do, he'll likely ask me more about mine, and I don't want to go into too much detail, considering what Lorelei told me about a new person in my life and all.

Our server arrives again with our drinks, and we realize we haven't even looked at the menu yet. Our server says she'll give us a couple more minutes and walks away. Garrick and I spend the time perusing the menu, and I try to decide what I'd like to order, all the while completely aware that I'm sitting just inches away from a man I not only find extremely attractive, but I'm developing a major crush on, too.

After our server returns, and we place our food orders, Garrick and I continue talking. Our conversation flows easily, and I find myself smiling and laughing a lot with him. When we hung out last night, we discovered that we share a lot of the same interests. Tonight, we're getting to know more about each other's lives, such as what our families and childhoods were like. I learn that he grew up in Portland and, like my parents, his still live in the same house. His only sibling is Sophie, who's three years younger than him.

Garrick is one year older than me. He graduated from the University of Oregon with an English degree and loves being able to travel the world and write about it for a living. His closest friend was his best friend growing up, who still lives in Portland, too. Garrick goes home to visit his parents as often as he can when he's not traveling or staying in Seaside to help Sophie, although he says he hasn't had time to make it over there in a while.

As we eat dinner, our conversation doesn't stop. He's fascinated to hear about my hometown, since it's such a different setting than where he grew up. He's never been to Port Townsend, and when he says he'd like to visit someday, I get excited, thinking about that possibility.

"Tell me more about your sisters," Garrick says. "What was it like to have four of you growing up together?"

I sit up a little straighter. I'm always proud to talk about my sisters. "We're all really close. Autumn is the oldest. She's two years older than me, and she lives in Portland. Well, actually, Beaverton to be exact. She works for Nike, which is why she moved down here to Oregon. Then, there's April, who's three years younger than me."

"Wait," Garrick says, and I wonder if he's caught onto our names. It's always fun to see how long it takes people to realize the unique theme our parents gave us through our names. "Your older sister is Autumn, you're Summer, and then there's April? Am I sensing a theme here?"

I chuckle. "You caught on pretty quickly." The next fun part will be when I tell him our last name. "Our parents named us after the season we were born in. Or, at least, a name associated with our season. Autumn was born in October, I was born in June, April was born in—"

"Let me guess," Garrick interrupts, but I melt at the sight of his sexy smile. "April?"

Nodding, I reply, "You got it. Mom liked the name April better than Spring, but Spring is her middle name."

"What's your middle name?" Garrick asks.

I giggle "June."

"Really?" Garrick's eyes widen, and I can't help but smile. "You're Summer June?"

I nod. "Yep. Summer June Seasons."

And there it is. The stunned look on Garrick's face tells

me he's trying to decide if I'm telling him the truth or fucking with him.

"Your last name is Seasons?"

I nod again. "It is! That's why my parents went with the first name theme. It worked perfectly with our last name, and once they started it with Autumn and me, they had to keep it going with my younger sisters, too."

"So, what's Autumn's middle name?" he asks.

"Margaret," I say, laughing again.

Garrick shakes his head. "Wait, wait, wait. She has a regular middle name?"

"Yes. It was our grandma's name."

"Ahh, that makes sense then," Garrick says with a chuckle. "Okay, tell me more. You still have another sister to tell me about."

"Holly is the youngest. She's five years younger than me, and she's the only other sister who lives in Port Townsend. In fact, we're roommates."

Garrick's eyebrows shoot up. "Is that right? That's cool. You must be close, even being five years apart."

"We are. All four of us are. Even though April lives in Seattle and Autumn's in Beaverton, we text and call each other all the time. We get together as often as we can."

"That's awesome. Your parents must be proud."

"They are," I reply. "Our family is close, and my parents have always been supportive of us. My parents are great. They've been married for thirty-five years, and they still act completely in love with each other. They're adorable together."

"That's sweet," Garrick says. "My parents are the same

way. They've been married for almost thirty-six years. Their anniversary is next month."

I smile. I have to admit, I'm relieved to hear his parents are somewhat similar to mine.

"I have one important question, though," he says, getting serious all of a sudden.

I cock an eyebrow. "What is it?" I ask, wondering what he wants to know.

"What's Holly's middle name?"

I laugh, and he joins me. "Noelle," I reply. "I bet you can't guess what month she was born."

"Holly Noelle," he says, putting his finger to his chin. "Could she have possibly been born in December?"

"Ding, ding, ding!" We laugh again, and I realize my cheeks hurt from smiling so much.

"I can't believe you're leaving tomorrow," he says, getting more serious. "We just met each other, and now you have to go back home."

It occurs to me that I never explained that I'm not going straight home when I leave Seaside. "Actually, I'm not going home tomorrow," I say, and I see a speck of hope in Garrick's eyes. "I *am* leaving Seaside, but I'm spending the week with Autumn at her house in Beaverton."

Garrick's smile widens. "You're going to be in Beaverton? That's great news!"

I laugh. He's so cute when he's excited. "Is it? I mean, I guess I'll be closer to Seaside, but—"

"I don't have to work Thursday or Friday," he says, and it suddenly dawns on me what he must be thinking. My heart pounds in my chest, anticipating what he's going to say next.

"I can drive to Portland for a couple of days to see you again... if you're interested."

Oh, I'm interested!

I smile wider, and my heart feels light. "I would love that," I tell him.

Garrick reaches across the table and takes my hand in his. "I like you, Summer. I'm glad we met."

His words make me blush. It's nice to know he feels the same as me.

Garrick pays our bill, and then we go for a walk on the promenade. It's a beautiful evening, and there are several beach goers enjoying the sunshine. Garrick and I continue talking about various things, and before we know it, we reach the end of the promenade.

"Want to walk back on the beach?" he asks, pointing toward the wide sandy path leading to the beach.

"I'd like that," I reply.

As we walk along the beach, Garrick surprises me when his hand reaches for mine. "Is this okay?" he asks, slipping his fingers between mine.

"Of course." I like the way his hand feels wrapped around mine. Warm, strong, and secure.

Our conversation continues as we walk back to where we started by the restaurant. By the time we get back, we've learned even more about each other. We stop to take in the gorgeous view splayed across the water. The sun is low in the sky, not quite ready to set, but it's still a beautiful sight to see.

"I love it here," Garrick says, watching the waves roll in.

"So do I. I love the beach. I can't imagine living away from it."

Garrick turns toward me. "Do you go to the beach a lot when you're home?"

"Not really," I say, realizing it sounds funny that I love the beach but hardly ever go, when I live right by Puget Sound.

"Why not?" he asks.

I shrug. "I guess because I'm usually too busy at home to enjoy the beach. I mean, once in a while, I'll walk along the waterfront, but it's really not the same. Here, it's the actual ocean waves crashing against the shore, and there's more beach to walk along. In Port Townsend, it's not the same. Don't get me wrong, it's beautiful, but it's different."

"I can't wait to see it," he says, and something about the way he says those words tells me he's serious. He's really going to make an effort to come to Port Townsend.

Garrick turns toward me, taking my hands in his. I look up into his blue eyes, hoping this is our moment. As he leans closer, my eyes instantly close. When his lips touch mine, I melt into him, and every muscle inside me clenches. I lose myself in this kiss as our lips move in unison, devouring each other. His hands slide up to my face, holding my cheeks, not letting me go—as if I'd want to break away from him.

No. There's nowhere else I'd rather be right now. Kissing Garrick is like heaven, and I have no intention of stopping.

But then he does.

"I have an idea," he says, looking into my eyes and brushing his thumb along my bottom lip.

I feel dazed. Like I've been put under some sort of spell. "What?" My voice barely comes out as a whisper.

Garrick cracks a smile. "Come on," he says, taking his left

hand in my right and leading me toward the promenade. "Let's build a bonfire and enjoy the sunset together."

And that's exactly what we do. Garrick purchases a bundle of firewood, a lighter, and even a fleece blanket from the Turnaround Market next to the promenade. Then, we find a good spot on the beach to build our fire. There are several other people in the area building bonfires as well. As he gets the flames started, I spread the blanket he bought out on the sand, so we have a place to sit. Garrick sits next to me as our fire crackles, the flames getting higher as it ignites the pieces of wood.

"This is perfect," I say. "The ocean, a fire... you..." I turn my head to look at Garrick.

He doesn't say anything. Instead, he presses his lips to mine and kisses me senseless again. His tongue glides with mine as we volley back and forth, not letting go of one another. My whole body responds to Garrick—I feel hot, my heart pounds in my chest, and I feel an ache at my core that I haven't felt in oh so long.

How can this be real? How did I end up here on the beach in Seaside, making out with one of the hottest men I've ever met? Things like this don't happen to me.

But then I remember—things may be easy with Garrick now, but how will things work out once I go back home to Port Townsend? He lives here, that is, when he's not traveling the world. How would we ever have any sort of real relationship?

I can't think about that right now. I want to live in the *now*, not get sucked into the mindfuck of worrying about the future. Lorelei told me to trust my instincts... well, every instinct in my body is telling me to enjoy this fling with Garrick, and that's exactly what I intend to do.

After watching the sunset, and sharing several more kisses while doing so, Garrick walks me to my car. We end our night with another passionate kiss before saying goodbye. As I drive back to the Sandy Shore Inn, all I can think about is the next time I'll get to see Garrick. Thursday. He's going to drive to Portland after work on Wednesday night, and he's going to take me out on Thursday. I only have four days to wait. That's not so bad.

* * *

I wake in the morning to the sound of my phone vibrating on the bedside table

next to me. I reach over to grab it and am pleasantly surprised to see a text from Garrick. We texted back and forth for a while last night after I got back to my room. He wanted me to let him know when I got back to the B&B safely, so I texted him when I arrived. Then, we didn't stop chatting.

Now, he's telling me good morning, and he hopes I have a nice drive to Autumn's house today. How sweet of him. It's nice to know that he's thinking about me, because he was the first thing on my mind when I woke up, too. My crush on Garrick has turned into so much more.

After I finish getting ready for the day and packing my things, I head downstairs to check out of the Sandy Shore Inn. I've enjoyed my stay here, and I'd love to come here again someday. The Mermaid Room isn't only a fun theme to sleep in, the bed is beyond comfortable, too. I've slept well here. The ambiance of this bed and breakfast, as well as

Lorelei's bright, magnetic energy, makes this place simply magical.

"How was your stay?" Lorelei asks from the other side of the check-out desk.

"It was amazing," I reply. "I don't want to leave, but I'm heading to Portland to visit my sister."

"Well, it was a pleasure to have you and your friends stay with us," Lorelei says, sliding my receipt across the counter. "You're always welcome here. And, don't forget..." She leans in as if she's letting me in on a secret. "Trust your instincts, Summer." She leans back and winks, smiling as if she knows something I don't... which, I suppose, is entirely possible with this woman.

"Thank you," I say, not knowing what else *to* say to her in this moment.

I fold the receipt and stuff it into my purse, then grab the handle of my suitcase and turn to leave.

"Love is in the air!" Lorelei's sing-song voice calls out, and when I turn back to look at her, she's already walking toward the kitchen, her flowy, green caftan dress flowing behind her.

Out of the corner of my eye, I see another person walking down the stairs. It's the blond woman I saw sitting alone, crying in the dining room as we ate breakfast yesterday. She's not crying now, so I hope things have improved for her. She notices me looking at her, which I realize must seem strange from her perspective, so I give her a quick smile and nod, then turn and head out the door.

I load my things in my car, then turn to look at the Sandy Shore Inn once more. I will definitely have to return to this place someday. But now, I need to get on the road and head to Autumn's house. I'm looking forward to spending time with her, as well as Holly and April, who will arrive at Autumn's house later tonight. The fun times of my week off work continue!

Just as I start my car, I get a text notification.

Drive safe and have fun with your sisters!

Instantly, I smile. I type out a quick reply and tell him I'll text him later today. Then, I put on my seatbelt, turn up the music on my stereo, and begin my journey to the Portland area.

Summer

Chapter 6

"You're here!" Autumn exclaims, swinging her front door open and throwing her hands in the air.

I walk up the steps to her front door. "I made it!" Once I reach her, I let go of my suitcase and wrap my arms around my sister in a warm hug. We haven't seen each other in a few months, and although we text nearly every day, it's not the same as actually getting to spend time together in person.

"Come in, come in," Autumn says as we let go of one another. Grabbing my suitcase, I follow her inside. "You're going to sleep with me, and April and Holly can sleep together in the guest room."

"Sounds good," I say, taking my things to her room. After getting settled, I sit at her kitchen counter while she makes each of us a cup of coffee. Autumn worked at a coffee shop all through college, so she takes her coffee making skills seriously. She has a full espresso machine in her kitchen, as well as several different flavored syrups to choose from.

While Autumn makes me a caramel macchiato, I type

out a quick text to Garrick to let him know I arrived at my sister's house.

"April and Holly will be here in a few hours," she says. "So how was Seaside? How are Michelle, Angela, and Penny doing?"

"They're good," I reply. "And Seaside was amazing. We stayed at the Sandy Shore Inn... have you heard of it?"

Autumn shakes her head as she stirs my drink. "No, I haven't. Was it nice?"

"It was amazing. We should take a sisters' trip and stay there sometime," I say as she hands me a cup of coffee.

"That would be fun. I love Seaside!"

"I didn't realize how close you really are to the coast," I say, taking a sip.

"Yeah, it's only about an hour and a half drive away. Cole and I like to go every once in a while."

"How is Cole?" I ask. The reason the four of us sisters are meeting here this week is to help Autumn with some of her wedding plans. She and Cole are finally tying the knot in December.

"He's good," she says. "He's in Chicago for work right now."

Unfortunately, I've only met Cole a handful of times over the nearly seven years they've been together. Cole has a demanding job working for a tech company, and he also travels a lot for work. The few times I've spent with Cole, he was always nice... but I've always wondered if he's the right guy for Autumn. I guess the fact that he finally proposed to her after openly admitting he has a fear of marriage is proof he truly loves her.

"How long is he in Chicago for?" I ask, wondering if I'll get to see him at all while I'm visiting here.

"He's flying back Friday. You might actually get to see him before you leave," she says with a laugh.

"Cool," I reply. "I haven't seen my future brother-in-law in a long time."

Autumn nods and takes a sip of her coffee. There's a hint of sadness in her eyes, and I wonder what that's all about. Before I can ask if everything's okay, though, she perks up and asks, "So, tell me... what's the latest gossip back home?"

I laugh. She always asks, and since Port Townsend is a small town, there's usually some sort of gossip to share. "Well, a new restaurant opened across the street from The Cellar that's giving it a run for its money. It's also in the basement of an old building and trying to go with the speakeasy vibe. Holly said Shawna is frustrated because not only are they copying the idea of The Cellar, but they also seem to be copying her menu."

"What? How can anyone do that? The Cellar is an institution in PT!"

I shrug. "The owners aren't local. Well, they are now, but they just moved to town from Bellevue. Word on the street is that they loved visiting Port Townsend so much, they decided to move here. They also own a restaurant in Bellevue, so they felt they could open a second successful business in PT... but so far, they're just rubbing all the locals the wrong way."

"Wow," Autumn says. "That's crazy. Shawna's dad opened The Cellar long before we were ever born. I can't imagine someone coming in and opening a copycat restaurant."

"Yeah, I'm sure Holly can tell you more about it when she gets here." Holly works part time at The Cellar.

Just then, I get a text notification. I pick up my phone off the counter and look at the screen. It's Garrick.

> I'm glad you arrived safe. You've been on my mind all day. Can't wait for Thursday!

"Who's that?" Autumn asks.

I type out a quick reply, telling him he's been on my mind, too, and I also can't wait for Thursday. "Oh, it's just a friend," I say to Autumn as I hit send, then set my phone down.

Autumn eyes me skeptically. "Really? What friend makes you smile like that when you read a text?"

Oops. I guess smiling the way Garrick makes me smile is a dead giveaway that I'm texting with someone who's more than just a friend. I guess I'll have to tell Autumn all about Garrick at some point, though, considering he's taking me out in a few days.

"Um... it's a guy I met," I admit, knowing I'm in for a full-on interrogation from my older sister.

Autumn's eyes widen, and she smiles. "Oh, really? Who is this guy? When did you meet? How could you not tell me about him before?"

I roll my eyes and reply, "Well, his name is Garrick. I actually just met him a couple of days ago in Seaside."

Autumn's eyebrows shoot up. "Wait, what? You met this guy in Seaside? When? Where? How?"

I chuckle at my sister's enthusiastic interest in my love life. "I met him on Saturday. He works at his sister's bookstore, which is where we met. Then, he showed up at the book signing VIP dinner we went to, and he and his sister ended up sitting at the same table as us, so we spent the evening talking. After that, we all went to the hotel bar and hung out more."

"Ooh, he works at a bookstore? He sounds right up your alley." Autumn waggles her eyebrows. "Is he cute?"

I nod. "Oh, yes." I suddenly wish I had a picture to show her. "Short brown hair, ocean-blue eyes... he's handsome. Fit, too."

"Nice. Did you see him anymore after that? What do you think's going to happen with him? I mean since he lives in Seaside and all."

I wish I knew the answer to her last question. "He took me out to dinner last night, then we walked along the beach and ended up building a bonfire and watching the sunset."

Autumn's eyes widen again, and her hand reaches across the counter to mine, shaking it in excitement. "Girl! That's so awesome! How romantic. Did you guys kiss?"

"Yeah, it was," I reply, unable to hide my smile. "And yes, we kissed. He's an amazing kisser."

Autumn can't contain her excitement for me, but suddenly, she gets a bit more serious. "Did you do anything else besides kiss?"

I shake my head no. "No, we didn't have sex, if that's what you mean. But..." I bite my lip, wondering what she'll say about this. "He's actually going to drive to Portland Wednesday night and take me out sometime on Thursday."

I swear Autumn's eyes are about to bulge out of her head. "He is? Holy shit, Summer, this is exciting!"

I try to laugh it off, but she's right. I'm very excited about what could be in store for Garrick and me... I just don't want to get my—or my sister's—hopes up too much.

My phone notifies me of another incoming text, and Autumn instantly asks, "Is that him again?"

I look at my phone and see his name on the screen. As I swipe the screen, I nod and reply, "Yep."

> The store is so slow today. I wish I didn't have to work. Have fun with your sister. I'll stop interrupting you with texts... although it'll be hard for me since I want to talk with you. Lol. Chat later.

Once again, his words make me smile. It's nice to know he wants to talk with me, but he also respects my time with my sister. I type out another reply.

> Sorry work is slow. Hopefully it picks up! I'll text you later... I want to talk with you, too!!! But feel free to text me if you want... I just may not respond right away if Autumn and I are busy. 😉

There. Hopefully, the winking emoji lets him know I want to talk to him, too.

"Oh, you've got it bad," Autumn says as I set my phone down again. "I can tell you really like this guy."

Surprised by her comment, I ask, "You can? How?"

"It's written all over your face. You can't stop smiling as you read his text and type out your own. Is this going to turn into a long-distance relationship for you two?"

My mouth drops, and I'm not exactly sure of the answer to her question. "I—I don't know yet. I mean, it's early to say, I guess. We'll see how things go on our date on Thursday."

"Well, it's something you should at least think about," Autumn says. "Because if Thursday goes well, you're going to have to figure out how and when you'll ever see each other again, considering you live so far away from each other."

"True," I say, knowing what she's saying is true, but also not wanting to get too far ahead of myself. Can't I just enjoy texting a cute guy and look forward to seeing him in a few days? I'll worry about the logistics of it all later... if I need to.

* * *

"We're here!" April announces as she and Holly walk into Autumn's house.

The four of us hug one another, excited to all be together again after so many months apart. Of course, I see Holly every day, and I've seen April more recently since she doesn't live *too* far away in Seattle, but it's been awhile since the four of us were all together.

After April and Holly set their things in the guest bedroom, we all gather in the living room. Autumn pours each of us a glass of wine, and we all get comfy on her couch and loveseat.

It doesn't take long before Autumn brings up that I've been texting a boy all day. Which is an exaggeration. We've only exchanged a few texts since he said he was going to leave me alone... which proved to be difficult for him to do. And I don't mind at all.

"So, he's a freelance writer?" Holly asks after I explain

who the guy is and how I met him. "What kind of writing does he do?"

"Yes," I reply. "He writes for travel magazines and websites."

"So, he travels a lot?" April asks.

"Wait!" Autumn suddenly gets excited. "Can we look him up online? Is his picture attached to any of his articles?"

Immediately, she picks up her phone. Why hadn't I thought of this before?

"Um, I don't know. I haven't looked," I say, picking up my own phone as well and seeing I have another text from him.

"What's his last name?" Autumn asks, ready to do a little online digging.

"Garrick Hyde," I reply, then spell it for her.

As she begins her search, and I anxiously await what she'll possibly find, I read Garrick's text.

What's your favorite kind of food?

I like all kinds of food. Why?

"Ooh! Is this him?" Autumn holds her phone out to me, and I take it from her hand to see what she found.

Sure enough, there he is. That gorgeous face I'm so damn attracted to is right there on the screen. I look at the article and see it's about Carnival in Brazil. He told me about this trip, and now I want to read this article.

"That's him," I reply as I read his writing.

"Let me see," April says.

"Me, too." Holly and April both move closer to me, hoping I'll show them the phone.

"Hang on," I say, wanting to read his article but quickly realizing I'll have to wait. I have three very impatient sisters. "Fine, here," I say, turning the phone around toward them.

"Oh, he's hot! Good job, girl," April says before going back to where she's sitting on the loveseat.

"Damn, girl," Holly says as she hands Autumn her phone back. "Lucky you."

Autumn takes a closer look at her phone before adding, "He's good looking, for sure. And he wrote this article about Brazil? How cool is that!"

I nod as I search for the article on my own phone so I can read it. "I told you guys he's attractive. Didn't you believe me?" I joke with my sisters.

I find the article and do a quick read of it as Autumn, April, and Holly discuss how they think he resembles country singer Sam Hunt. I'm only half-listening, but I can't disagree with that observation.

"So, he just travels the world and writes for a living?" April asks. "And works at his sister's bookstore?"

"Must be nice," Holly says. "Maybe he'll take you on a trip with him someday."

I'm only halfway through his article but pull my eyes away from my phone to look at my sister. "It's too soon for that," I say, although I have to admit that would be pretty awesome.

If things end up progressing between us, that is.

"How does he make enough money to make a living and travel so much?" April asks, and I get the feeling she's somewhat skeptical about Garrick.

Setting my phone down, I reply, "He lives with his sister in Seaside when he's there. I don't know exactly how much money he makes doing freelance writing, but between that and the bookstore, he must make enough. I mean, he seems to be doing well for himself."

"Fair enough," April says with a shrug. "It's just not a common career you hear about every day, so I was wondering."

I nod, but I can't help but wonder now—is he just mooching off his sister when he's not traveling? I hate to think of him as a freeloader, but April's right—it's not your everyday common career.

I try to shove those thoughts aside as another text from Garrick comes through. I open it up to read it.

> Cool. I have an idea for our date on Thursday. Do you like Greek food?

> I love Greek food!

"So, I have some news I want to tell you all about," April announces, finally changing the topic off me.

"What is it?" Autumn asks.

"I told Holly already on our drive down here," she says, and Holly smiles smugly at Autumn and me, like she knows a secret we don't... which is actually the case. April continues, "I've been chosen to move onto the next round for an upcoming reality show."

I nearly drop my phone.

"What?" Autumn screeches.

April nods. "You have to keep this a secret," she says. "Otherwise, I could be kicked out of the running if they somehow find out I'm telling people this... but you're my sisters! How can I not tell you?"

Still stunned by her news, I say, "Of course, you can trust us. What show is it?"

April had told us months ago that she was considering applying for dating shows to help her find 'the one,' so I have a feeling it's one of those.

April smiles sheepishly before saying, "Meet Me at the Altar."

My mouth drops open as Autumn screeches again, "What?"

April nods. "If I make it past this round of interviews by the production team, I'll move onto the final round, which consists of meeting the marriage counselors who work with the contestants. If they feel I'm ready for marriage, and if they're able to find a good match for me, I'll be on the next season of the show."

"Holy shit," I say, completely surprised by my sister's news. "You mean to tell us you could be marrying a *stranger* on a reality show?"

"I mean, it *is* one of the more successful reality shows, in terms of couples who stay together. But, again, I need to make it past two more rounds before I find out if I'm actually going to be on. I'll keep you all posted on how things go."

"Do Mom and Dad know?" Autumn asks. I'm wondering the same thing, although I highly doubt she's told them yet.

April shakes her head. "No, and I'm not going to tell them unless I make it on the show. So, please don't say anything."

"Your secret's safe with all of us," Autumn tells her, and Holly and I agree.

* * *

Later, after many glasses of wine over pizza and good conversation with my sisters, we decide it's time for bed. However, before I make it to Autumn's bedroom, I receive another text from Garrick, telling me good night. After I reply, he responds again, and before I know it, I'm curled up on the couch with a comfy blanket around me, texting the guy I like.

> I'm glad you had a fun day with your sisters. I have to admit something, though...

> What's that?

My heart pounds as I wait for his reply. What is he going to admit to me? Is it something good? Bad? God, I hope it's good.

> I can't stop thinking about you. Holding your hand, kissing you. I can't wait to see you again on Thursday.

I suck in a breath as I read his confession. It's good. Really good.

> I can't stop thinking about you either. I had such a good time with you in Seaside, and I can't wait to see you... and kiss you again.

> Damn. I wish I could drive to Portland tomorrow.

> Me, too. Although I'm going dress shopping with my sisters tomorrow, so I'll be busy anyway.

> I hope you have fun. I have to work, too, so we'll just have to wait. I wanted you to know that you're on my mind, though. I like you a lot, Summer.

I can't stop smiling. However, suddenly, April's question from earlier comes to mind, and I wonder about his job. Not only that, but another thought comes to mind—when is he taking another trip? We already live so far apart from each other; how will a relationship work with this man if he's constantly traveling around the world to make a living?

I hate that I'm thinking ahead like this, assuming we'll end up in a relationship together already. I need to remember that I just met this guy, and we're just getting to know each other. I deserve to have a little fun... and that's what I intend to do this week. I *am* on vacation, after all. If things end up working out with Garrick, I'm sure we'll figure things out.

> I like you a lot, too, Garrick. I can't wait for Thursday!

> It's getting late. Are you in bed?

> No, I'm on the couch. I have to share a bed with Autumn tonight, and she went to bed. So did Holly and April, so I'm the only one up.

I see the dots moving, telling me he's typing something, and I wonder what he's going to say next. When his text comes through, and it's a selfie of him lying back against his pillow in bed, looking sexy as hell, I nearly lose it. He's not wearing a shirt, although I only see the top of his shoulders, not his entire chest. This man is gorgeous, and I can't believe I get to go out with him again in a few days.

I decide to reply with a selfie of my own, so I take the best picture of myself I can, then send it to him.

> You're beautiful. I want to kiss those lips again.

My belly flutters when I read his words. He thinks I'm beautiful and knowing that feels good. I need to tell him I feel the same way about him.

> Thank you. I think you're handsome. I'm so attracted to you, and I can't wait to kiss you again, Garrick!

"What are you doing?" Autumn's voice makes me jump, scaring me half to death, and I drop my phone on the floor.

"Jesus," I gasp as I see her standing at the entrance to the living room. I lean over and pick up my phone.

"Are you texting Garrick?" she asks, a knowing smile on her face.

I feel myself blushing. "Maybe..."

"Well, don't let me interrupt you," she says as I stand and walk toward her. "I was just checking to see if you had fallen asleep out here or something."

"No, I'll come to bed now," I say, suddenly feeling silly.

"Why? Don't let me spoil your night."

I look at the time and see it's almost midnight already. We have plans to go out to breakfast in the morning, so I shouldn't stay up too much later anyway. "I'll just say good night to him, and then I'll come to bed."

"Okay. But, really, you can stay up as long as you'd like," Autumn says, then gives me a quick hug before turning and walking back toward her bedroom.

I turn my attention back to my phone.

> You have no idea how happy it makes me to know you feel the same way about me that I feel about you. I'm so glad we met each other!

> I was just thinking the same thing! I'm so glad I met you, and I can't wait for Thursday. I'm getting up early in the morning, though, so I need to go to bed now. Sleep well! Talk tomorrow! 😘

I head to Autumn's room and get ready for bed. Before I go to sleep, I see one
last text from Garrick.

> 😘😘😘

God, I hope Thursday comes quickly!

Garrick

Chapter 7

"You're here!" Mom greets me at the door with open arms, and I embrace her.

"Hi, Mom. It's good to see you," I say just as Dad appears in the entryway.

"Hi, son," he says as I walk in the door. I give him a hug as well. "How long are you in town for?"

"I got in last night," I say as we walk into the living room and sit to visit. "I'm heading back to the coast Friday night."

"I'm glad you came to visit. We haven't seen you in a while," Mom says, and I instantly feel a little guilty for not making more of an effort to see them when I'm in Oregon.

"I know, and I feel bad about that. Sophie has needed help at the shop during the busy season, and I just get so wrapped up in that, it's hard to break away."

"We haven't seen Sophie in a while either," Mom says.

"Now, Nora," Dad says. "Both Garrick and Sophie are busy. We can't expect them to drop everything to come visit us all the time. We could make more of an effort to go to Seaside once in a while, too."

Dad always thinks more rationally. He's right, although I know I should visit my parents more often than I do. It's not that I don't want to spend time with them; life just gets busy sometimes.

"I know, I know," Mom sighs. "I just miss seeing my kids around."

Oh, the Mom guilt.

"I'll try to come around more often, Mom. I promise. And I'll tell Sophie, too." There. Hopefully, that'll make her feel a little better.

I look at Dad, who rolls his eyes at me, although Mom can't see. I silently chuckle to myself. I love my parents.

"So, what are your plans while you're in town?" Dad asks. "Did you come to Portland just to get away or for something specific?"

I knew my parents would ask this, and I don't want to lie to them, but I also don't want to get their hopes up that I'm going on a date. "I'm meeting up with a friend tonight," I say, which isn't lying.

"Oh, which friend? Colin?" Mom asks, referring to my oldest friend since childhood.

I hadn't thought this far ahead in my plan of withholding the truth from my parents. They're friends with Colin's parents, so if I say I'm meeting up with him, chances are Mom will talk to his mom and say something about us getting together while I'm in town... and then Colin's mom will likely say something to him about it... which will lead to my lie being exposed.

Crap. I feel like a frickin' teenager again, trying to get away with something I shouldn't be doing. This is silly. I'm thirty-one years old. I should just tell my parents the truth and not let their inquisition bother me. After all, they must know I date once in a while... right?

"Um, no, not this time. I'm actually taking a woman out on a date."

Mom's eyes light up, and Dad's eyebrows hit his hairline.

"Oh, really?" Mom says, sounding hopeful. "Who is she?"

"Someone who came into the bookstore last weekend. We hit it off. I took her out while she was still in town, and I decided to drive over here to take her out on a second date."

"So, she lives in Portland?" Dad asks.

"No, actually," I chuckle. "She's visiting her sister in Beaverton for the week. She lives up in Port Townsend, Washington."

"Port Townsend? Isn't that way up there on the peninsula?" Dad asks.

I nod. "Yeah, it's kind of far from here."

"Well, she must be something special if you drove all the way over here to take her out again," Mom says, and I know that's her subtle way of digging for more information about her.

I chuckle. "Yeah, she's a nice person, and we have a lot in common. Don't get ahead of yourself, though... it's only a second date. I was apprehensive to even tell you guys about it because I don't want you getting the wrong idea."

"Hmm," Mom says, eyeing me skeptically. "Okay, okay... but I know you, Garrick. You don't like to waste your time, and you don't go on many dates, so she must be something special."

Dad places his hand on hers. "Nora, we only know about

the dates Garrick chooses to tell us about. He probably dates more often than we know."

Jesus. Why is this turning into a thing? I should've known better. And, no, Dad I don't actually date that often... but I'm not going to let them know he's right.

Time to change the subject.

"So, how was Aruba?" I ask, referring to the recent vacation they took two months ago.

"Oh, it was fun!" Mom picks up her phone off the coffee table. "Let me show you the photos I took. Come here." She pats the couch cushion next to her, and I move to sit by her.

As long as we don't have to talk about my dating life anymore, I'll look at as many vacation photos she wants to show me.

* * *

A few hours later, I've said goodbye to my parents, cleaned up for my date, and I'm on my way to meet Summer at the Greek restaurant I love in the Pearl District of Portland called Eleni's. Although I offered to pick her up, she preferred to drive herself and meet me there instead.

After all the text messages we've shared over the past few days, I can't fucking wait to see her again. We've flirted —a lot. I'm so damn attracted to her; I have butterflies in my stomach. Sure, both times we hung out together we got along great, and our banter back and forth this week has all been great. But I can't help but worry that things with Summer will somehow fall apart. It's the pessimist in me. The fact that we live so far away from each other is a hurdle we'll have to get over if we want a relationship

together. Not to mention my job that has me traveling the
world off and on throughout the year. There's a lot to
consider if Summer and I are going to continue things after
this date.

Just as I arrive at the restaurant, I get a text from Summer
saying she's waiting inside. Thank God I won't have to wait
for her to arrive.

As I open the door, I see her right away, waiting in the
foyer. Her face lights up in a gorgeous smile, and I can't help
myself—I walk straight over and embrace her.

"It's so good to see you," I say, realizing how good it feels
to have her in my arms and for her arms to be wrapped
around me.

"It's good to see you, too," she says, her breath tickling
my neck.

Reluctantly, I step back, but I don't want to let go of her,
so I slip my hand into hers. She seems surprised, but she
looks at me and smiles, telling me she doesn't mind.

The server seats us at a table right away, and we're quiet
as we both look over the menu. I haven't been here in quite a
while, considering I haven't spent much time in Portland
lately. "Everything here is delicious," I tell Summer. "You
won't be disappointed with anything you order."

"That's good to know," she says with a smile before
looking back at her menu.

After our server returns, and we give her our order,
Summer and I turn our attention toward each other. "How
was your day?" I ask. We've texted each other some today, so I
kind of already know, but it's a good conversation starter.

"It was good. We helped Autumn research possible
venues for her wedding, so that was fun. Then, April and

Holly left to go back home, so we said goodbye to them a couple of hours ago."

"Did you help Autumn pick a place?" I ask.

She shakes her head. "No, but we narrowed it down to four possibilities. She's going to take her fiancé to each of them to take a look, then they'll decide together."

"Cool. Were you sad to say goodbye to Holly and April?"

"A little," she replies. "I mean, Holly's my roommate, so I'll see her when I get home in a couple of days. I don't know when I'll see April next, but we see each other pretty regularly. She comes home to visit Port Townsend quite a bit. It's Autumn who I barely get to see, so I'll be sad to say goodbye to her on Saturday."

"That makes sense," I say. I love that Summer is so close with her family. Some of my exes didn't have very good relationships with their families, so it's refreshing to meet someone who seems to have a similar type of relationship I do with my own parents and sister.

"So, I have a question for you," Summer asks, folding her hands on the table in front of her.

"Ask away," I say, curious what she wants to know.

"Is this our second date or our third? Because we spent last Saturday night at the VIP dinner and went to the bar afterward, but we were also with your sister and my friends."

I chuckle and rub my chin. "That's a good question. I suppose we could count that as a date, although I'm not really sure it constitutes as a real one." I hadn't considered Saturday night as a date, although we did get to know each other pretty well that first night together. I wonder why she's asking.

"Okay. I was just wondering," she says with a laugh.

Then it dawns on me. Third dates usually have more expectation behind them... as in, a lot of people consider the third date to be the first time they sleep together. Is that why she's wondering?

"Is there any particular reason you're wondering?" I ask, and she blushes.

"No... not really. I was just curious what you thought."

With the amount of flirting we've done this week via text messages, we've gotten pretty close to crossing the line into the sexting category. To say I wouldn't have sex with Summer tonight, if she wanted to, would be a lie. Hell, if she asked me to meet her in the restaurant's bathroom right now, I'd do it. Our chemistry is strong, and there's no doubt I'm sexually attracted to her.

Our server returns with our drinks, and then our conversation changes topics. She asks how my day was, and I tell her it was good to hang out with my parents. I leave out the part about telling them about our date tonight. No reason to bring that up, or how my mom would love to see me settle down sooner than later.

Our conversation flows easily as ever, and by the time we finish eating dinner, I feel like this should count as our third date. I want Summer. I want to take this relationship to the next level with her. I know things will be complicated with where we live and what I do for a living, but I don't want this to be the last date we ever have together.

I need to take my shot with her. I need to handle this smoothly, too. After our server clears our table, I lean my elbows on the table and decide now's as good a time as any. "So, I'm curious," I say to her. "Do you still consider this our second date, or would you say this is more like our third?"

Summer cocks an eyebrow. "I don't know." She leans her elbows on the table and smirks at me. My dick strains against my pants. "Considering this is the third time we've gone out together, and that we've spent every day this week texting each other practically nonstop—" she licks her lips, the innocent gesture turning me on even more— "I'd say this is definitely more of a third date for us."

"I can't disagree with that logic," I say, smiling. We hold each other's gaze for a moment before I continue, "Would you be opposed to going back to my place?"

Summer's eyebrows knit inward, and she looks confused. "To your place? You mean your parents' house?"

Confusion washes over me at first, but then it dawns on me. I never actually told her I have my own place here. She must've assumed I'm staying with my parents while I'm in town.

I chuckle and shake my head. "No, not my parents' house. *My* place. I guess I never told you this, but I have a condo here in Portland."

Her mouth drops. "You do?" I nod, and she follows it up with another question. "But, why? I mean, I thought you traveled the world and lived with Sophie in Seaside when you were home."

"I can understand why you thought that. I never fully explained things to you." I don't usually divulge this information until I absolutely need to with women. Otherwise, I never know if they like me for me or for what I have. "Here's the thing. I have my home base here in Portland. When my grandparents passed away, both Sophie and I inherited money from them. She bought the bookstore and her house in Seaside, and I bought my condo. I do stay with Sophie whenever I'm in Seaside, but that's usually just this time of year when she needs extra help at the store. The rest of the year, when I'm home, I live here."

Summer just looks at me, not saying a word. I can't tell whether she's mad or not. I hope she's just processing all this information I dumped on her. I suddenly feel bad for not being totally truthful with her before, and I feel like a fool that I didn't mention it sooner tonight before asking her to come back to my place.

Finally, she says something. "So, you inherited money and bought a condo and live here when you're not traveling, except for when you help Sophie in Seaside?"

I nod, hoping she's understanding and doesn't tell me to fuck off. "I'm sorry I didn't tell you this sooner. I honestly don't know why I didn't."

Summer clears her throat. "And here I thought you were like a vagabond, traveling the world and mooching off your sister when you weren't." She scoffs.

Her comment makes me chuckle. "You thought I was a mooch? And you still liked me?"

She rolls her eyes. "I was giving you the benefit of the doubt. After all, I thought it made sense. You travel for a living, so why would you have your own place?"

I laugh. "True. I get it. But, believe me, I'm not mooching off my sister. I help her pay the bills when I stay there, so I'm not freeloading."

Summer eyes me as if she's trying to figure me out. I wish I knew what she's thinking. I pray she's not going to tell me to have a good life and leave.

Finally, a slow smile spreads across her face. "I like you, Garrick. I really do."

"I like you, too," I say, reaching across the table and taking her hand in mind.

She looks down at our joined hands. "Where's your condo?" she asks, looking up at me through her lashes.

Fuck, she's sexy.

"Not too far from here," I say. "I actually walked."

Her eyes widen, and I can tell I've shocked her once again. "You live in the Pearl District?"

I nod, hoping she still wants to come home with me.

She shakes her head. "You are full of surprises tonight, aren't you?" She pauses and looks at me as if she's thinking things over. My cock twitches, I want her so bad. "So, should I leave my car where I parked it or would it be safer to drive it to your place?"

I breathe a sigh of relief. "That depends. Where did you park?"

"In the garage at the end of this block," she says, pointing in the direction of my building.

"You can leave it there. It's close enough, and you may not find a closer spot anyway. I only have one parking spot in my building's garage, unfortunately."

After I pay our bill, we leave the restaurant hand in hand, and I lead us back to my condo. It's a short walk, and as soon as Summer sees my building, I can tell she's surprised once again. By the time we make it up to my place on the eleventh floor, I think she may die of shock. As we walk in, she stops in her tracks before making a beeline across my living room to my floor-to-ceiling windows that look out across the city.

"This is your view?!" Summer is clearly astonished. She turns around and looks at me. "*This* is your condo? How much money did your grandparents leave you?"

I chuckle and walk across the room to meet her. "My grandparents were well off. They left both Sophie and me a good chunk, and this is what I chose to buy."

Summer turns to look out the window again. "This is incredible. You can see Mount Hood and everything!"

It is an incredible view, but all I want to see right now is Summer. In my bed.

I take her hand in mine, and she turns toward me again. I look into her blueish-green eyes, and my free hand strokes her hair. "You're so beautiful," I tell her before lowering my head to hers and kissing her soft lips.

Summer's mouth moves with mine as she places her free hand on my waist. I let go of her hand and cup her cheek. She lets out a soft moan at the touch.

"I want you," I whisper. I lick her bottom lip before kissing her again.

She doesn't say anything, but she doesn't have to. As soon as her hands move to the front of my shirt and begin unbuttoning it, I know she feels the same way.

Summer makes quick work of my shirt, and I help by taking it off and dropping it to the floor. She places her hands on my chest and just looks at me for a moment before saying, "God, you're sexy." Then her lips are on mine once again.

We continue undressing one another until we're both wearing nothing but our underwear. She looks incredible in her matching black bra and panties, but I don't get to enjoy it long before she reaches behind her back to unclasp her bra. She drags the straps down her arms, exposing her voluptuous, perky breasts, her hard nipples begging to be touched.

I reach for her, taking her in my arms and kissing her hard. My hands explore her soft skin as she does the same to me, rubbing her hands over my chest, down to my stomach, and then lower to my boxer briefs. As my hand skims over her breasts, her hand cups my cock, rubbing the silky material still covering it.

I moan into her mouth. My fingers toy with her nipple, and she moans as well before pulling down my boxers. My cock springs free, and her hand wraps around it immediately, slowly stroking it up and down as I pinch and pull her nipple. I don't care if we're standing in front of my window. It's still light out, but no one can see us up here, as we're in the highest building within viewing distance.

Our tongues slide against each other in a constant battle of give and take. Neither of us lets up, even when I walk us toward the sofa. Once we're there, I force myself to let go of her, but only so she'll sit on the brown leather.

"Sit here," I tell her, and she follows my direction. I kneel down on my knees and reach for the waistband of her underwear. As I pull them down, I also pull her so that her butt is on the edge of the couch. She leans her head back as I slide her panties down her legs, then drop them on the floor. I spread her legs and prop them up on my shoulders. "You have a pretty pussy," I tell her, stroking my finger along the folds.

She squirms. "That feels good," she mews.

I rub her clit for a while, watching her enjoy what I'm doing to her. Then, I replace my finger with my tongue and push my finger deep inside her. She moans at the contact and begins counter movements against me.

"Yes... yes!" She moans with pleasure as she gets closer and closer to release. "Don't stop."

So, I don't. I keep licking and sucking her bundle of

nerves and insert a second finger, driving her wild. Before long, her inner muscles contract, and she calls out in pleasure.

I stop what I'm doing and look up at her, completely sated, lying back against the back of my couch. Her eyes slowly open and look at me. "You taste so good, baby," I say, then suck on my fingers, wet with her juices.

"That's fucking hot," she says before sitting up, taking my head in her hands, and kissing me hard and fast. When she pulls away, she wipes her mouth and says, "I wanted a taste, too."

Holy fuck. If I wait any longer, I may come before I even get the chance to sink my dick in her. Quickly, I retrieve a condom, dispose of my boxers, and slide the rubber onto my shaft. "Lie back," I tell her, and she turns her body and lies back against the length of my couch.

I crawl over her, and she spreads her legs, giving me full access. I press my lips to hers and kiss her senseless as I push my cock into her wet pussy. Her back bows, and she moans as I go balls deep, then rear back and move at a delicious pace. She feels so good... *more* than good... I'm afraid I won't last as long as I want.

I trail kisses down her neck to her chest, then lavish her nipple with my tongue. She moans in pleasure, so I suck it in my mouth while rolling the other one between my fingers.

"Don't stop," she says in a breath.

Oh, I don't intend to.

I feel my orgasm building too soon, though, so I know I need to do something to make this last longer. I slow my movements and move my head up. "Ride me," I tell her, hoping she'll comply.

She nods. I sit up so she can move, sitting back against my couch. Summer straddles me, and I grab her hips to help guide her into place. *Perfect.* This position is good for more than one reason. Not only will it help me last longer, but from this angle, her tits will be right at level with my mouth.

Summer sinks onto my cock, and my head falls back. "You feel so good," I tell her. "Your pussy is so nice and tight."

She moves up and down, and I can tell this position is better for her as well. Her head falls back, and she fondles her own breasts. It's a fucking sexy sight—this beautiful woman fucking me, touching herself as she's getting off on it all. When she suddenly screams out, "Yes!" and I feel her pussy contracting around me, I know she's coming again.

Summer slows her movements, and I move her hands, holding them so I have access to her breasts. I suck, pull, and lightly bite as she rides me faster again. As I feel myself getting closer, I let go of her hands so I can rub her clit with one and fondle the breast I'm not pleasuring with my mouth with the other.

As I get closer to release, I move my hips with her, pushing in as deep as I can possibly go. I watch Summer as her eyes close, enjoying all the sensations going through her body. She's so gorgeous... so perfect... I hope this won't be the only time we ever get to have sex together.

We continue moving at a steady pace, and I press against her clit, causing her to flood my cock as she calls out my name in ecstasy. Hearing my name on her lips does it for me, and I moan in pleasure as I pour myself into her.

As we both recover, breathing heavily and wiping the sweat from our foreheads, I look at Summer. Like, *really* look at her. Yes, she's beautiful. Yes, she's sexy. But I realize in that moment, it's not just about that with her. I feel more than just a physical attraction toward her—I feel an emotional connection, too.

Summer smiles, then kisses me sweetly on the lips before standing, gathering her clothes, and getting dressed.

"That was good," I say, watching her move gracefully around my living room.

"Yeah, it was," she replies, reaching behind her back to clasp her bra.

"Don't go." The words come out of my mouth before I give it a second thought.

Summer stops and looks at me. "You want me to stay?"

"Of course. I don't want our date to end like this. I wasn't looking for a wham-bam-thank-you-ma'am type of situation. I want to spend more time with you."

She blushes, her lips lifting in a smile. "I want to spend more time with you, too."

Those are the words I was hoping to hear.

Summer and I both get dressed. She stands at my windows, looking in awe at the beautiful view. With the sun setting now, the sky has a pink hue to it. "This is unbelievable. I can't get over this," she says, pointing at the view in front of us.

I wrap my arms around her and kiss her forehead. "Yeah, it is," I whisper.

Although Summer doesn't know, I'm not just referring to the view. I'm referring to us and the relationship I want to continue with her. I need to figure out how to make that work; I know I'm not going to get over my feelings for Summer anytime soon.

Summer

Chapter 8

I wake up, wrapped in silky sheets, lying in one of the most comfortable beds I've ever slept in. As my eyes focus, I see Garrick, still sleeping soundly next to me. I can't get over how handsome he is and how attracted I am to this man. And now... now we've taken our relationship to the next level, and it was fantastic.

Seriously. I haven't had sex like this before. It's as if Garrick knows exactly where and how to touch me to make me come. And come I did... multiple times. I've never had a partner like Garrick before, that's for sure.

After our first romp in the living room, we watched as the sun went down over Portland, and the view was magnificent. I'm still shocked that he lives here. He owns this condo, as in he paid for it outright. He doesn't have a mortgage. His grandparents must've been extremely wealthy if they were able to leave such a hefty sum to both Sophie and Garrick like this. I don't know how much this condo cost him to buy, but Autumn's fiancé rents an apartment somewhere in the Pearl District as well, and she's told me how expensive his rent is each month. I can only imagine a place like this cost a fortune.

Suddenly, I'm filled with more questions about Garrick's life. What did his grandparents do to make so much money? Are his parents rich, too? Although he told me about his childhood, he never made it sound like he grew up with a lot of money. It seems as though Garrick is extremely humble, and that only makes me like him more.

But I'd still like to find out the answers to my questions and learn more about his life. I'll have to ask him later and hope it doesn't offend him in some way.

I get up and pad over to the bathroom. Thoughts of last night fill my mind, remembering how wonderful everything was. After we enjoyed the view, we decided to watch a movie on TV, settling on *Forrest Gump,* which happens to be a favorite for both of us. It was nice to cuddle together on the couch while we watched it, and as soon as it ended, we decided to go to bed.

But we didn't sleep. Oh, no. Garrick and I had sex again, and it was even better than the first time.

After using the bathroom, I crawl back into bed. Garrick stirs and then wakes up. He instantly smiles when he sees me, which makes my belly muscles clench. The effect this man's charm has on me is unlike anything I've experienced before. Sure, I've gotten butterflies in the past when a boyfriend would look at me a certain way, but to get that more intense, sexual pull feeling just from a single look is different.

"Good morning," Garrick says.

"Good morning," I reply, then lean over and kiss him briefly on his lips.

"Mmmm. I like that." Garrick's voice is a little deeper,

more gravelly than normal, probably because he just woke up, and I find it sexy as hell. "Did you sleep well?"

I nod. "Your bed is so comfortable. I'm jealous you get to sleep here all the time. Or, I guess, at least every time you're in Portland."

"Yeah, I splurged on a nice mattress," he says with a laugh, and I can't help thinking *the mattress isn't all you splurged on,* considering his entire condo is furnished well. "You're welcome to sleep here whenever you want," he adds, pulling me closer to him.

"I am?" I ask, combing my fingers through his hair.

"Yeah. I wish you could stay here with me again tonight." He plants a kiss on my forehead, then my nose, then my lips. "But I'm not even staying here tonight. I have to drive back to Seaside today."

Pouting my lips, I reply, "I wish we could stay here again tonight, too."

"I was thinking," Garrick says, and I get excited about what he could possibly say next. "I could drive up to Port Townsend next week to visit you for a few days."

His words light me up inside. My entire body feels like it's buzzing, and I can't wipe the smile from my face. I'm so excited to hear that I won't have to wait very long to see Garrick again.

"You can do that? What day will you come up?"

"I can ask Sophie for an extra day or two off. Now that the Seaside Festival is over, business should be slowing down a bit, so I'm sure she won't mind. It's not like she doesn't have other employees who can fill in if needed, too."

"Okay, if that works. I'll feel bad if it puts Sophie out, though."

Garrick shakes his head. "No, I know it won't be a problem. Don't worry. I'll talk to her when I get back tonight and let you know what day I can drive up to see you. I know you have to work next week, but at least we can spend the evenings together."

I kiss him. I don't care if we both have morning breath. Garrick has made my day—no, my week—actually, it's now becoming more than that. I didn't expect to meet a guy I liked so much and had such incredible chemistry with when I went to Seaside last weekend, and I didn't expect things to progress with Garrick the way they are now. I was happy without a man in my life, but Garrick is adding to that happiness, filling me with pure joy.

"Text me when you get to Autumn's house, just so I know you made it there safely," Garrick says as we embrace one another. I don't want to let him go, and I don't want his strong arms to let go of me.

"I will," I reply, breathing in his musky cologne scent that I like so much.

Garrick presses his lips to mine, our bodies flush against each other. I lose myself as we kiss each other passionately, not holding anything back. I need this. *We* need this before we go our separate ways for a week. It's crazy to think a person can suddenly become so important in your life like Garrick has in mine. We didn't even know each other a week ago, and now it's hard for us to say goodbye to each other.

Reluctantly, we pull apart from one another, but not

before he kisses me sweetly once more. "I should get going," I say. "I know you have to leave soon for Seaside, too."

"Okay. Text me. And I'll text you."

We kiss one more time before he steps back so I can get in my car. He had walked me to the parking garage I left my car in overnight, which was only a block away from his building.

I start my car, then roll down the window. Garrick leans in and kisses me again. "Drive safe. Do you know how to get back on the freeway from here?"

I grab my phone from my purse and hold it up. "Navigation will tell me."

"Okay. Give me a call if you get lost," he says with a smirk.

I laugh as I plug my phone in, then type Autumn's address into the map app and click on the directions. Once it's ready, I set my phone down and turn back to Garrick. "Thanks again for last night."

"You're welcome. Thank *you* for last night." He winks, then leans in and kisses me one last time before he steps back from my car so I can leave. I roll up my window, then put my car in reverse to pull out of the parking spot. As I drive away, I look in my rearview mirror to see the kindest, sexiest man get further and further away from me.

Damn. I hope he can come to Port Townsend early next week.

It doesn't take long for me to drive to Autumn's house. When I had texted her to let her know I was staying at Garrick's last night, she was happy for me. She also said that she and Cole were going to look at a couple of the venues this morning and early afternoon, since they both have the day off. She said they would be back by two o'clock, though, and it's now three, so she's back already.

Autumn's car is in the driveway when I pull up, but I don't see Cole's car. I was half-expecting him to be here when I returned, but I'm really not surprised that he's not. Elusive Cole strikes again.

Her front door is locked, so I knock. It doesn't take long for the door to open, but I'm not expecting to see Autumn look the way she does. Her eyes are red, watery, as if she's been crying. "Hi," she says, her voice shaky.

I'm filled with concern as I walk inside. "What's wrong? What happened?" I ask, stopping in the entryway.

Autumn closes the door and turns toward me. "It's Cole. We got in a fight about wedding venues." She shakes her head as if she's trying not to cry again. "It's stupid, really. I don't know why I'm so upset about it."

"It's not stupid," I say, giving her a hug. "Tell me what happened."

We make our way into the living room and sit on the couch. "We went to two of the venues on my list today. The first one was the golf club in West Linn, and the second one was McMenamin's Edgefield."

"And, what, he didn't like them?" I ask, wondering what could've happened.

She laughs, fighting back tears. "You could say that. He said the golf course was okay, but he thinks it's too far away for any of our friends and family to go to." She rolls her eyes. "It's really not, but whatever. So, then, I felt silly driving out to Edgefield since it's all the way out in Troutdale, but he insisted we still go and check it out. Well, he then proceeded to be completely unimpressed with it, telling me he doesn't understand why I thought it would be a good place. He thinks the space they have for weddings is too small for us, it's too far away... any little thing he could come up with to complain about, he did. We ate lunch there, and he complained about the service *and* the food, which I didn't have a problem with at all. He was really just being a dick, Summer."

"I'm sorry," I say, trying to comfort her. "He must've been having a bad day."

She sniffs and wipes her eyes. "Yeah, I guess so. I can't believe he was so rude, though. I mean, you saw both venues online. *All* of the venues we looked at were fabulous, don't you agree?"

I nod. "Yes, they were. Any of those places would be perfect for your wedding."

"I know, right? I don't understand why he thought they weren't good enough." She shakes her head. "He can be such a snob sometimes, I swear. He likes having high-end things, so I guess he's expecting our wedding to be at someplace over-the-top expensive."

I put my hand on Autumn's shoulder, trying to comfort her, but I'm unsure of what to say. "I'm so sorry."

Honestly, though, this whole situation has me questioning if Cole is really the right guy for my sister. I haven't spent enough time with the guy to know him well enough, and everything Autumn just told me makes him sound like a complete ass. Now, I'm worried my sister may be making a huge mistake marrying Cole.

Autumn wipes her eyes again and forces a smile. "Enough about this," she says. "Tell me about your date last night!"

As excited as I am to tell her about Garrick, now I feel like this isn't the right time. She's mad at her fiancé for being a jerk, and now I'm supposed to brag about what a great guy I've met? This doesn't seem right. I need to downplay it a little.

"It was fine... not exactly what I expected, I guess..."

"Really? But you stayed..."

I shrug. "I mean, it was good... It just sucks because he lives here when he's not in Seaside or traveling the world. I don't know how things will end up working out between us."

Although I'm trying to downplay how great my date was, everything I said is the absolute truth. The reality of the situation is that things really do suck in terms of a future with Garrick.

That thought is depressing and puts a damper on the great mood I was in just a short time ago.

"Well, I guess you can just enjoy things for now and see where it goes. Maybe you'll find a way to make things work," Autumn says, and I appreciate her attempt at trying to lift my spirits.

Wait—aren't I supposed to be lifting hers right now?

"Thanks," I reply, now wanting to shift our conversation away from talking about Garrick and me. "So, what should we do tonight? It's my last night in Portland. We should do something fun."

Autumn's eyes light up. "Should we go out for dinner and drinks? Or would you rather stay in, get dinner via Door Dash, and watch a good movie?"

Smiling, I reply, "Door Dash sounds perfect. I'm going to change into pajama pants and a t-shirt."

"Perfect!"

Garrick texts me later to let me know he made it back to Seaside safely. We text off and on all evening. I like him—like, *really* like him—but reality has set in, and I don't want to end up getting my heart broken. Sure, he's planning to come visit me next week, but then what? Are we going to do that every week? Once a month? As much as I want things to progress with Garrick, I'm not sure how we're going to make things work in the long run.

Shit.

$Summer$

Chapter 9

"I have some news," Holly says, walking into the kitchen and tossing her purse onto the counter.

"Oh?" I press the pre-heat button on the stove and give my attention to her. She just got home from a day of subbing at the elementary school. I've only been home for about twenty minutes after working a long day myself, and I'm opting for an easy dinner tonight—cooking a frozen pizza.

Holly tries to hide her smile, but she can't contain herself. "Patrick asked me to move in with him."

Her news takes me by surprise, but only a little bit. "Wow! I'm assuming you said yes?"

She nods. "Yes, but I also told him I had to talk to you first. I'm not going to leave you in a bind with the rent here."

Oh, sweet Holly.

Shaking my head, I reply, "No, no. I'm fine. Sure, it helps to have a roommate who pays half of everything, but the truth is I can afford it on my own. I'll be fine."

Holly rounds the counter and wraps me in a hug. "Thank you, sis," she says. "I've loved living with you, and

I'm thankful you let me move in when I came back home. I'm going to miss you."

"You're very welcome, but you don't need to thank me. I've loved living with you, too. It won't be the same without you here, but I'm sure we'll still see each other plenty. It's a small town."

We both laugh, then step away from each other. "Are you making pizza?" Holly asks, noticing the pizza box on the counter.

"Yeah. Easy peasy. Want some? We can open that bottle of wine," I say, nodding toward the bottle of malbec also on the counter.

"Sure. I'll have a little before I leave, anyway. I'm going to pack," she says, starting to walk out of the kitchen.

"Wow, you can't wait to get out of here, can you?" I laugh.

"I'm not packing to *move* yet," she says, stopping in the doorway to the living room. "I'm just packing for the next few days."

"I know, I know. I appreciate you staying with Patrick while Garrick is in town," I reply, although it's not unusual for Holly to stay at Patrick's house anyway. She stays with him most nights of the week on a regular basis these days. "You're not leaving until Garrick gets here, though, right? You're going to meet him first?"

"Yes, of course," she says. "I don't want to miss out on meeting your new man." She winks before heading out of the room.

* * *

A couple of hours later, after Holly and I have devoured almost the entire pizza, I've had a couple of glasses of wine, and she's sipped on one, there's a knock on the door. "He's here!" I practically squeal like a little girl. I've been looking forward to this moment for five days.

Garrick and I have spent the past five days talking and texting, getting to know each other more, and my feelings for him have only grown. It's crazy how much things can change in such a short amount of time. It's only been five days since I said goodbye to him in the parking garage near his condo, but it feels longer. When he told me that Sophie gave him Wednesday afternoon off so he could leave earlier in the day for his drive here, rather than having to close the store, I was elated. I also thought we were only going to have a couple of days together, but Sophie ended up giving him a couple of extra days off, too, which means Garrick doesn't have to head back to Seaside until Sunday.

I swing the door open and find Garrick standing on the other side, looking even more handsome than the last time I saw him. Instead of his five o'clock shadow look, he has a full beard. I never knew I could be so attracted to a man with facial hair, but I'm ready to skip introducing Garrick to Holly and take him straight to my bedroom.

"Hi, baby," he says as we wrap our arms around each other, kissing each other on the lips.

I don't care if Holly is around the corner, waiting to meet Garrick. I melt into him and savor his touch. The smell of his musky cologne hits my nostrils and goes straight to my libido. Who knew a scent could turn me on so much.

"It's so good to see you," he says before kissing me again.

"Mmmm," I say, reluctantly pulling back because I know

we should go in the house. The sooner we do, the sooner Holly will leave to go to Patrick's house, and the sooner we'll be alone. "Come inside. I want you to meet my sister before she goes to her boyfriend's."

Garrick picks up his suitcase and follows me into the house. As we walk into the living room, Holly stands and puts her hand out toward Garrick. "Hi, I'm Holly. It's so nice to finally meet you!"

He shakes Holly's hand. "It's a pleasure. Summer has told me so many wonderful things about you and your other sisters, too."

"Ah, that's nice to hear. I'm her favorite, though," she says with a wink.

"Oh, Holly... of course you are," I say with a laugh.

"How was your drive up here?" Holly asks Garrick, and I'm curious to know, too.

Garrick rubs the back of his neck. "It was long, but it was also a beautiful drive. I love traveling and exploring new places, and I've never been to this part of Washington before, so I enjoyed it."

"It's definitely a beautiful part of the world," Holly says. "I hope you enjoy your time here. I'm sure Summer will show you what a fun town Port Townsend is."

"I'm looking forward to it," he says, looking at me with a warm smile.

"Well, I hate to leave so soon," Holly says, grabbing her purse off the table, "but I'm heading out now. Patrick is expecting me, and I know the two of you would like to have some alone time." She winks at me as she walks toward the door, grabbing her suitcase where she left it by the hallway on her way.

"It was nice to meet you," Garrick says.

"It was great meeting you, too," Holly replies, then looks at me and gives a little wave. "Have fun. See ya later!"

"Bye. Say hi to Patrick," I say as she walks out the door.

As soon as the door shuts behind her, Garrick and I turn toward each other. It takes about 1.2 seconds for us to pounce on one another. We're clearly both on the same page, not wanting to wait any longer than we already have to be with each other again.

"I want you," Garrick growls as he pushes my hair back.

I answer him by crashing my lips on his again. I claw at his shirt, and he helps to remove it. "Bedroom," I say, taking his hand in mine and quickly leading him down the hall to my room. I close the door behind us. If Holly forgot something and comes back to get it, I wouldn't want her to walk in on us.

Garrick faces me, and his lips curl in a sexy smirk. He reaches for my shirt and pulls it over my head. My heart pounds in my chest. I want him so much; it's surreal to finally be back together with him after imagining how this moment would go.

We claw at each other's clothes until we're both stripped down, and then he pushes me onto the bed, crawling over me and kissing me on the lips again. Our hands roam each other's bodies. He sends goosebumps down my side as his hand grazes my skin before taking my nipple between his fingers.

"Mmmm," I moan. Although he's not touching it, my clit throbs. I try to release the pressure by rubbing against his leg, but instead, his hand trails down from my breast and spreads my legs apart. Then, his hand is there, rubbing my pussy in all the right places, and I feel nothing but pure pleasure.

"You're so wet," he says, breaking our kiss. He lowers his head and sucks my nipple in his mouth, intensifying my pleasure and making me squirm.

My hands roam his body, trying to get a hold on his cock, but I can't reach it from this angle. Instead, I lightly claw his back. When Garrick pushes a finger inside me, my nails dig into him more, and he moans. "Sorry," I say on a breath and lighten the pressure on his skin.

His head pops up long enough to say, "Don't apologize. Mark me if you want. I like it."

As he swirls his tongue around my hardened nipple, the feeling shoots straight to my clit again. My head falls back against my pillow, and it doesn't take long before that familiar tingling sensation starts. Before I know it, my body comes apart. "Yes!" I call out as my body shakes, my muscles clenching around Garrick's finger as he continues to push in and out, prolonging my pleasure.

He slows his movements, then moves down on the bed. "I want to taste you," he says, settling between my legs. I pop my head up and watch as his tongue swipes against my pussy. The sight of him turns me on. As I lie back against my pillow, I claw at my sheets. Every lick of Garrick's skilled tongue gets me closer to another release, and before I know it, I'm coming apart again.

As my body relaxes, Garrick gets off the bed. I look to see what he's doing, and I see him retrieving a condom. It's a sexy sight to see him put it on, holding his cock in his hands as he slides it onto his hard length.

Once he's got it in place, he looks up and notices me watching him. His lips curl up. "Are you ready?"

I nod, unable to form words at the moment.

"Do you want me to fuck you?" he asks with a wicked grin as he moves back onto the bed.

My mouth goes dry, but I find my voice. "Yes," I say as he crawls over me. I lie back against the pillow and look into his eyes.

"You're beautiful," he says, pushing the hair out of my face again. "I've dreamt about doing this again for the past five days."

"So have I," I say, and then his mouth is on mine again, kissing me sweetly.

But it quickly becomes more passionate than sweet. Our tongues volley back and forth as he lines his cock up with my pussy. My back arches off the bed as he pushes in deep, and I moan in pleasure.

Garrick doesn't fuck me, though. He's gentle and sweet, caressing my body and kissing my lips as our bodies move as one. It's not how I expected this to play out, considering we were ravenous with each other a few moments ago.

As Garrick makes love to me, he hits that spot deep inside over and over again, pushing me closer to the edge. I claw at his back, knowing I'm leaving marks now, but not caring since he doesn't. I'm teeming with the need to release. I rock my hips up, hoping the change of angle will get me there, and it does. As I fall over the edge, I call out Garrick's name.

Later, after I've come two more times, the last time along with Garrick, we lie together in my bed. His hand lazily draws lines up and down my arm. I'm too tired to move anymore. Sex with Garrick is good, but it's also a workout. I've never had a partner last so long and pleasure me multiple times before finishing. Don't get me wrong—I'm definitely *not* complaining, but I may need to start working out again to keep up with him.

"I'm so glad I'm here," he says, then kisses my neck below my ear, sending goosebumps down my body.

"I am, too." I turn my head and kiss him. As our tongues swirl together, a thought comes to mind. I break our kiss and ask, "Are you hungry? Did you stop to eat anywhere on your way?"

"Oh, I ate," he says with a smirk. His hand travels down to the apex of my thighs, and his finger swirls my swollen clit. "I may get hungry for seconds later, though." I gasp at his touch. It wouldn't take long to bring me to another orgasm, but his hand is gone too soon. Instead, he sits up. "Seriously, though, I'm starving. I haven't eaten since lunch."

I sit up, too. "You must be starving. I have pizza I can reheat for you, or we can get something else."

Garrick stands and slides on his boxer briefs. "Pizza sounds good. I'm hungry, but I'm also tired and don't feel like getting back in the car right now." He chuckles. As he continues to pick up his clothes to get dressed, I notice the faint scratch marks I left on his back. It's a bit of a turn on knowing I marked him... a visual reminder of when he was pleasuring me.

Although I know he's kind of joking about not wanting to get back in his car, there's also truth to what he said. It took him four hours to drive here. Four hours! How are we ever going to make a long-term relationship work when there's such a long distance between us?

I stand and get dressed as well, trying not to dwell on that discouraging thought. He just got here; I want to enjoy my time with Garrick, not think about the difficulties we'll face *if* we decide we want to continue our relationship. Who knows where things will go with him? I need to remind myself I don't need to have all the answers right now. What I need to do is enjoy my time with him and live in the *now*. We have the next four days together, and I intend to make those the best four days I've ever spent with a man.

Garrick

Chapter 10

"It's so beautiful here." I'm in awe of the view, looking across the sound from the pier Summer and I are standing on. Although it's early in the morning, the sun's rays are already beating down on us, and my skin feels moist from the humidity. I didn't expect it to be quite so hot, but apparently, there's a heat wave hitting the Pacific Northwest, and the temperature is supposed to hit triple digits this afternoon. It's already in the high eighties.

"What mountain is that?" I ask, pointing at the white-speckled peak in the distance far across the water.

"That's Glacier Peak," Summer replies. "And that—" she points further north at another mountain poking out— "is Mount Baker."

"Incredible. Of all the places I've been around the world, this definitely makes the list for one of the most stunning."

Maybe this is a good time to tell her. I've been avoiding this conversation ever since we met because I don't want the news to have any sort of effect on our relationship. But I can't continue to avoid it much longer.

Unaware of my inner thoughts, she replies, "Really? Wow. I mean, I knew Port Townsend is a beautiful place, but I never considered it to have one of the top views in the world."

I can't bring myself to do it yet. I know as soon as I tell Summer my news, things will change between us. I haven't even been here twenty-four hours yet, and I want us to enjoy our time together first. Not only that, but Summer also has to go to work soon, so I don't want to put a damper on her day before it even gets started. We woke up early and came down to the waterfront to get breakfast at a cafe before she has to be at work.

I put my arm around Summer's shoulder. "I'm so glad I drove here last night. It was worth getting up early to have breakfast with you before you have to work today."

"Aw, thanks," she says, leaning her head on my shoulder and wrapping her arm around my waist. "I'm glad you came up last night, too."

"What time do you have to be at work?" I ask, glancing at my watch.

"I'm due there at nine," she replies casually. Under normal circumstances, I'd point out the pun in what she just said, considering she works at the library, but she must not realize how late it is already.

"Uh, you better get going then," I say, dropping my shoulder and showing her the time on my watch. "You only have ten minutes!"

"Oh, crap!" She looks at her own watch, as if it's going to say a different time. "Sorry—we need to go!"

We speedwalk back to her car, which, luckily, is only parked a block away. Then, she drives me back to her house, which is where I'm going to hang out while she's at work. If I feel the need to go anywhere, I can always drive myself, although I don't really have anywhere to go. My plan is to do a little writing on my travel blog. I haven't posted any updates in a while, and I know I should.

I've also been kicking around the idea of writing a book the past couple of years, but I haven't actually had the down-time with absolutely nothing else to do to start brain-storming ideas for it. When I'm at home, I always have something else keeping me busy. Here, I won't have anything else to do while Summer is at work, so I plan to use the time to my advantage.

As we turn onto her street, Summer says, "Sorry again that I have to work while you're here. I wish I didn't, but I had all of last week off."

"It's okay, babe. It's really no problem." I reach over and take her hand in mine, and she glances at me with a smile on her face.

"I'll be home at about five thirty. I'll give you my key in case you want to go anywhere." She pulls up to the curb at her house, then reaches for her keychain, carefully taking one of her keys off the ring and handing it to me. "Here you go."

"Thanks," I say, taking it from her, then leaning over and kissing her. I intend for it to be a quick peck on the lips since she's going to be late for work, but she grabs the back of my head, keeping me there, prolonging our kiss. As our tongues glide together, I touch her cheek and lightly rub my thumb back and forth. I'm falling head over heels for this woman.

She pulls back and looks at me. "Have a good day. Text me if you're bored. I'll respond when I can."

"I will," I say, then unbuckle my seat belt and exit the car.

Before I close the door, though, I lean over and look back inside at her. "Have a good day. Don't work too hard."

"Thanks," she says, and I close the door.

I watch as she drives away. I look at my watch and see she has about five minutes to get there. Hopefully it's a short drive for her. It probably is, considering Port Townsend isn't that big of a town, but I still hope she's on time.

I let myself into Summer's apartment, which is one of three units in an old Victorian style house. It's a beautiful home, and her apartment takes up the entire main floor. It's a nice place in a quiet neighborhood that's not too far from the downtown area. So far, I like it here in Port Townsend. I hope I get the opportunity to come back and visit Summer again someday.

I get my laptop out and set myself up at her kitchen table. I make myself a cup of coffee, then get to work.

"Honey! I'm home!" Summer's voice calls from the front entryway, followed by the sound of the front door closing.

I walk into the living room to greet her. "Hi, babe," I say, walking straight over to her for a kiss.

"Mmmm," she says as we pull apart. "I like coming home to this."

I'm not sure if she means she likes getting kissed when she comes home, or she likes coming home to me, but I'm fine with either of those meanings. The truth is, I like her coming home to me. I'm not going to say that aloud, though.

"Are you still writing?" she asks. We texted a few times throughout the day, so she knew what I was working on.

"Yeah, I just shut my laptop down. I set myself up at your kitchen table."

"Oh, perfect," she says, kicking her shoes off and leaving them next to the coffee table.

"I want to take you out for dinner," I say, hoping she's not too tired to go out.

She smiles. "You do?"

Nodding, I reply, "Yes. I've been thinking about it for the past couple of hours. You choose the place, and I'll buy you dinner. Anywhere you want to go."

She cocks an eyebrow. "Anywhere, huh?" She smiles. "I know just the place. Let me freshen up a bit, and then we can go."

"Perfect," I say. She kisses me again before walking down the hall toward her bathroom.

Ten minutes later, we're on our way to dinner. This time, I drive. She instructs me where to go, and it doesn't take long for us to arrive in the historic downtown area, not far from where we had breakfast this morning. I find a place to park, then we walk hand in hand toward the building with a mermaid sign hanging above the door.

"Here we are," Summer says, leading us into the doorway. "All the way up the stairs. This place has the best view and some of the best food in town."

We walk up the stairs, then down a hallway and around a corner to the entrance to Mermaids Pub & Grill. We walk inside and see that the place is pretty busy. The sign says to seat ourselves, so I follow as Summer leads the way outside to the balcony.

"Well, shoot," she says as we look around and see all the tables are taken. She's right about the view. It's the same as the view we had on the dock this morning, only from a higher point. "I guess we'll have to sit inside. Hopefully, we won't have to wait too long."

I follow her back in, and she leads us through the bar to another room on the other side. There's a pool table in the middle of this room with several tables and booths around the perimeter. Luckily, we spot an empty table and snag it for ourselves.

"I can't believe how busy this place is on a Thursday," Summer says. "I mean, it's always packed on the weekend, but I didn't expect so many people to be here tonight."

"It's okay. We got a table, so it's all good."

"I'm surprised so many people are sitting outside, too, considering how hot it is," she adds.

I laugh. "What do you mean? You wanted to sit outside, too!"

She laughs and shrugs a shoulder. "I know. I mean, I guess it's cooled down enough to be tolerable. I'm glad I was inside with air conditioning all day."

"Me, too. I'm glad your apartment has AC."

Our server arrives, welcomes us, and gives us menus before walking away again. Summer and I look over the menu, and once I've decided what I want, I look around at all the eclectic artwork hanging on the walls. A large painting on the opposite wall catches my eye. It's a naked woman lying on a chaise lounge. But then I notice she's not alone. There's not one, not two, but four men surrounding her, as if they're worshiping her. One's kissing her foot, one's touching her arm, another is behind her head, and one is kissing her thigh. As I study the painting further, I realize the four men have horns on their heads, like they're devils.

"That's an interesting piece of art," Summer says, noticing what I'm looking at.

"Yeah, it is," I say. "I just noticed the naked lady has four devils surrounding her."

Summer looks at the painting again. "Oh! I see it now! That's kind of... hot..."

Her comment takes me by surprise. "Is it?"

She blushes. "Yeah... I mean, she's just lying there naked, and those four devils are worshiping her body. It's kinda hot."

I wasn't expecting Summer to say that. We've only had sex a few times together so far, and by no means is she sweet and innocent in the bedroom. But for her to find this piece of art *hot* makes me wonder what else turns her on. Is she more of a freak in the sheets than she's letting on? What kinds of sexual experiences has she had in the past?

Leaning my elbow on the table, I ask, "Would you like to be that woman, lying on a chaise lounge looking all sexy, with four men worshiping your body?"

Summer looks at me and giggles. "No... I mean, I'm not into having orgies, if that's what you mean." Her eyes widen a fraction before she asks, "Why? Are you?"

I laugh. I can't help it. I think I've actually scared her a bit, and that wasn't my intent. "No, no. Although, I'll admit... I had a threesome once."

Her eyebrows shoot up, and I can tell I've totally shocked her. "You have?"

Nodding slowly, I reply, "Yeah... it was several years ago. I was in France. I know it sounds like a cliche, but when in Rome... or, rather, when in Paris..." I shrug, not sure what else to say about that one.

"Wow," she whispers, still stunned. "I—I've never done that before."

I put my hands up, wanting to explain myself. "That's perfectly fine and trust me—I'm not going to ask you to do that. It was a one-time deal for me, and it's not something I'm dying to do again. So, you don't need to worry."

She relaxes a little and smiles again. Then, our server returns and takes our order.

After we finish eating, I convince Summer to play a round of pool. I'm shocked to discover how skilled she is at the game, and even more shocked when she beats me. "I can't believe how good you are! I had no idea you're a pool shark!" I say as we walk back down the long staircase on our way to my car.

Summer laughs. "Why are you surprised? You don't think a librarian could possibly be that good at a bar game?"

"Well, no... it's not that... I just really didn't expect you to be that good. I've never been beat by a woman before."

"Oh, so you just didn't think a *girl* could be that good? A sweet, fragile *female*? What is this, 1951?"

I laugh. She's got me there. I sound like a misogynistic asshole now. "No, no, no!" We stop walking, and I turn toward her, taking her in my arms. "I'm really not a sexist dick. I'm sorry I underestimated your pool-playing skills. I'm impressed with how good you are."

Summer glares at me, but I can tell she's only pretending to be upset. Her eyes soften, and her lips curl up. "Well, don't ever underestimate me again, okay? You never know what I'm capable of." Her lips land on mine, and we kiss. I hold onto her tightly, pressing my body against hers.

A passerby reminds me we're in the middle of the sidewalk, and I reluctantly pull my lips back. "Let's go back to your place. I've been wanting to take you to bed all day."

Summer smiles. "Is that right? Well, you're in luck because I've been wanting to take *you* to bed all day." She takes my hand in hers. "Come on. Let's go."

We walk the short distance to my car and get in, then I drive us back to her place. I know I need to have the difficult conversation with Summer sometime before I leave here on Sunday, but tonight's not the night. Maybe tomorrow... or maybe I'll wait until Saturday. There's no need to rush it. I want to enjoy these last few days with Summer before I tell her everything I need to get off my chest.

Summer

Chapter 11

"I love this place," Garrick says, sitting back in his chair, taking in the view.

I relax in my chair and look out across the green field as well. It's Saturday, Garrick's last day in Port Townsend, and we decided to go wine tasting. This is our second stop of the day, at Port Townsend Vineyards. We chose to sit outside since it's another lovely day, although not as hot. It's only in the low nineties.

I take a sip of the Riesling in my glass. "This is good wine," I say.

"Yeah, it is," Garrick agrees. "This was a good idea. Thanks for bringing me here."

"Of course," I reply. "I wish you didn't have to leave tomorrow."

"Me, too," he says, then takes another sip of wine, although this time he chugs the rest of his glass, then sets it on the table between our two chairs. He turns toward me, leaning his elbows on his knees. "Summer, I have a couple of things I need to tell you."

My stomach knots up. Based on his body language and choice of words, I have a feeling I'm not going to like what he's about to say. After all the fun we've had the past few days, getting to know each other on deeper levels, the great sex we have... what the hell kind of bomb is he going to drop on me now?

"What is it?" I ask, praying it's not as bad as he's making it out to be.

He lets out a breath before continuing, "Well, to begin with, I want to tell you the truth about my job."

The *truth* about his job? He's been *lying* to me all this time? I don't understand, since I read some of his articles online. The hairs on the back of my neck stand on end, and I hold my breath in anticipation of what he's going to say.

Garrick nervously rubs his forehead, then he looks at me. "Summer, everything I told you was true. I'm a freelance writer who travels the world and writes about my travels. You also know it's true that I help Sophie at her bookstore when she needs an extra hand. I never lied to you about anything, but there *is* something I *didn't* tell you."

I can hear my heartbeat in my ears. "What's that?" I ask, only it comes out as a whisper.

"I didn't just inherit enough money from my grandparents to buy my condo. I get paid from a trust fund every month, too."

The beating in my ears stops as I stare at Garrick. The handsome man who came into my life so unexpectedly has left me speechless. I'm filled with a mix of emotions, and I don't know where to start.

He reaches over and places a hand on my knee. "This isn't something I go around bragging about. I only tell people on a need-to-know basis. I wanted to make sure you liked me for *me* before I told you. I've learned the hard way not to tell women too soon... you'd be surprised how many gold diggers there are out there."

I open my mouth to defend myself. I'm not a fucking gold digger! But then I consider what he's just said to me. He trusts me. He waited to tell me to make sure I like him for who he is, not for what he has. I close my mouth, still unsure of what to say.

"My grandparents were very wealthy," he explains. "My grandfather started his company in his twenties, and it took off. They were able to leave millions for my parents, Sophie, and me. I feel very fortunate, and I don't take it for granted."

My mind is racing with questions, but I finally find my voice. "What was your grandfather's business?"

"Butterfield Chocolates," he says, and my mouth drops open.

"Your grandfather created Butterfield Chocolates?" This is unbelievable. Butterfield Chocolates is a household name. "Are you being serious right now?" I'm literally dumbfounded by this news.

Garrick nods. "I'm completely serious. My mom's dad was Charles Butterfield. That's her maiden name. She's the only child of the founder of Butterfield Chocolates."

I stare at Garrick, stunned. "So... you're a millionaire?"

Garrick slowly nods. "Yes."

As reality sets in, I have nothing but questions. "Who runs the company now?"

"No one in my family runs the business anymore. My grandfather sold the company to a larger food manufacturer a couple of years before he passed away. In the deal, they agreed to keep the original recipe as well as the name."

"Wow," I say in a breath. "This is a lot to take in."

"My grandfather didn't want Sophie and me to get all our money for nothing, though. Sure, we each got a huge chunk of money right away. I used mine to buy my condo, and Sophie used hers to buy the bookstore. But for us to collect our monthly trust money, Sophie and I have to hold down jobs of our own as well. It doesn't matter what kind of job it is; we just have to have some sort of employment; otherwise, we won't collect our monthly payment."

That's interesting.

"So, as long as you have a job, no matter what it is, you also get extra money each month?" I lean in closer to him and ask, "How much do you get?" Immediately, I regret asking. "I mean, you don't have to tell me. I shouldn't have asked. That's too personal."

Garrick chuckles. "No, it's okay." Then he leans in and whispers, "I get ten grand a month."

I have to pick my jaw up off the floor. "I'm sorry, did you say *ten grand*? You get ten grand every month?" My mind is spinning. Garrick is *rich*. Really fucking rich. It doesn't make a difference to me—I mean, obviously I liked him before I knew this—but now that I do know, this sort of changes things. I'm sure he's never had to worry about money before in his life. As long as he has some sort of job, no matter how minimal it is, he collects his monthly trust money. This explains how he's able to maintain such an extravagant condo in Portland and travel all over the world.

"I know you're surprised," he says. "But yes, that's how much I get every month. I don't spend it all, though. I put some away in a savings account, and I also invest a little. I don't want it all to disappear and be left with nothing later in life."

"Will your trust fund payments eventually run out?" I ask, curious about how these trust funds work. I have no idea since no one in my family has ever been rich enough to establish one.

"Well, no," he says with a chuckle. "I just want to make sure I don't throw all my money away. Plus, I mean, who knows if ten grand a month will be enough to live on in thirty or forty years. I don't want to be in my seventies and not have enough money to live off."

Fair enough. Garrick is clearly smart with his money, and the fact that I had *no* clue about his wealth attests to how humble he is, too.

I look at Garrick and shake my head. "I'm shocked. You've shocked me with this news."

"I thought you would be, but I had to tell you," he says. "It explains why I get to do what I love. I can travel the world, write about it, get paid a little for each article, but not worry about how much I'm getting paid because it's not my main source of income."

"I'm jealous," I say, thinking how amazing it must be not to have to worry about money. "I mean, I do love my job, and I do make a decent living, but it sounds like you're living the dream."

"I guess I am," he says.

Another thought comes to mind. "So that's how Sophie was able to buy her bookstore and become a successful small business owner at such a young age."

He nods. "Yeah. It was always a dream of hers to own a

bookstore at the beach. She made a smart investment and bought a business that makes her a good income on top of the amount she gets from the trust. She's able to stash a lot away each month and splurge on things she enjoys."

Clearly, Sophie and Garrick don't fit the spoiled trust fund baby stereotype.

"That's amazing," I say. "What a wonderful gift your grandfather left you."

"I'm forever grateful to him," he replies.

I look back out at the view of the field in front of us and take a sip of my wine. Garrick's news is a lot to take in. I'm dating a guy who's rich. Like, really, really rich.

Holy shit.

I'm still trying to adjust to this news when Garrick says, "I have one more thing I need to tell you."

My heart stops, and I look at him, nervous about what bomb he's going to drop on me now. "What is it?" I ask, hesitantly.

Garrick rubs his forehead, then lowers his hand and looks me in the eye. I get the feeling this news isn't as good as his last bombshell. "My next trip out of the country is less than a week away. I'm leaving for Australia next Friday."

As I comprehend what he just said, my heart leaps to my throat. "*Australia?*"

He's leaving for Australia in six days? Why didn't he mention this trip before? "How long will you be there?" I ask, hoping it's not for *too* long.

"About a month."

For the second time in a very short amount of time, I'm stunned. "*A month?*" I practically screech.

"I know it's a long time. I've never been to Australia

before, and I'm going to travel all over the country while I'm there."

Jesus. I guess if you're traveling all the way to Australia, you should make the most of your time. But I'm not ready to say goodbye to him for a month already. As fast as everything has progressed between Garrick and me, I didn't expect things would come to a screeching halt for us so soon.

"When will we get to see each other again?" I ask.

"I don't know," he says. He looks down and shrugs. "I'd like to keep in touch and get together again after I return to the States. But I don't expect you to wait for me."

Again, my mind spins with all of this new information being dumped on me. What does he mean? He doesn't expect me to wait for him? "What exactly do you mean by that?"

Garrick looks at me again, his expression sadder than before. "I mean, if you want to go on any dates while I'm gone, you should. Don't wait around for me to get back."

Confusion washes over me. "You want me to date other people?"

"Well, no, not exactly," he says. "But I also don't expect you to put your life on hold for me while I'm out of the country."

I don't know what to say. I thought our relationship––as new as it still is––has been getting stronger. I'm falling for Garrick. I don't want to date anyone else right now.

Then another unpleasant thought comes to mind.

"Wait—are *you* planning to date other women while you're in Australia?" His story of having a threesome while he was in France springs back to mind. Suddenly, I feel sick to my stomach.

"What? No!" Garrick looks at me with sincerity in his eyes. "I have no plans to date anyone. I like you, Summer. I like you a lot, and I want to continue what we've started and see where it goes. I hope you'll want to see me again when I return from my trip, but I also don't want to be a selfish prick and expect you to wait for me."

I take a deep breath and try to organize all my thoughts so that what comes out of my mouth sounds coherent and not crazy. "Garrick, I like you a lot, too. I know we've only known each other a short time and we haven't exactly established what our relationship is yet, but I want to see where things go with us. I have no intention of dating anyone else while you're gone."

Garrick's lips curl up, and he looks relieved to hear me say that. "I feel the same way about you."

I let out a breath I didn't know I was holding. Garrick's words warm my heart, and I feel relieved his feelings mirror mine.

After hitting a couple more wineries, then having dinner at The Cellar, we've come back to my place. We can't keep our hands off each other and end up in bed. Garrick's fingers lightly stroke my arm as we lie together in post-coital bliss.

I wish he didn't have to leave tomorrow, especially now that I know he's leaving the freakin' continent for a month. I know we don't live near each other anyway, but a four-hour drive is a lot closer than... wait, how far away *is* Australia, anyway? I know a flight takes something like eighteen hours...

"How far is Australia?" I ask. "I mean, I know it's far, but what's the time difference?"

Garrick kisses my shoulder before answering, "Sydney, where I'm flying to, is seventeen hours ahead of us."

"Holy shit," I say, trying to do the calculations in my head.

He kisses my shoulder again, then his body seems to still for a moment, and I wonder why.

Before I can ask what's wrong, he says, "Come with me."

Now, *my* body stills. "What?" I ask, unsure if I've heard him correctly.

"Come to Australia with me," he says.

My heart races. I want to roll over so I can see him, but I'm still frozen—frozen in fear. Going to Australia with Garrick would be a *huge* step in our relationship, and I'm not sure we're ready for that yet.

"You want me to go to Australia with you?" I ask. "Like, just pack up, leave my job and everything here behind for a month?"

"Yes."

I force myself to roll over and look at him. I touch his cheek, his beard soft beneath my fingers. "Are you serious?"

He nods. "I'm going to miss you. I don't want to wait so long to see you again, and it would be fun to have you join me."

"I have to work, though," I say, moving my hand down to his shoulder. "I can't just drop everything and leave."

His mouth turns down, as if he forgot I have responsibilities I can't just abandon at the drop of a hat. "I know, it was a crazy idea. I understand... but I'd love it if you could."

"I wish I could," I say, and it's the truth. How amazing

would it be to travel to Australia? I've never left the continent of North America before, so that alone would be
incredible. Traveling with Garrick and being alone with him
for a month would be beyond belief.

"I wish you could, too," he says, then kisses my forehead.
"We'll have to plan another trip together someday."

The thought of that fills me with hope. Hope that our
relationship will survive him being seventeen hours away for
a month and hope that things will progress between us once
he returns.

Summer

Chapter 12

Twenty-four hours later, after turning down Garrick's offer to travel with him, I'm lying in my bed again... alone. Garrick left several hours ago, and he has just called to let me know he arrived back in Seaside. We talked for a while on the phone before we said good night, and now here I am, all by myself again.

I liked having Garrick here the past few days. I'd gotten used to sleeping with him next to me, and now my bed seems too large without him. I'll have to wait over a month before I get to sleep beside him again.

If there was a way I could go to Australia with him, I would. However, I can't just take a month off work, especially at the last minute like this. I'd have to quit my job to go, and I don't want to do that. Not only do I love my job, I don't want to let my colleagues down. Financially, I also need to keep my job. I have rent and bills to pay, so it's kind of crucial for me to stay employed.

I really wish I could go with him, though.

As I fall asleep, all my thoughts are of Garrick. In the

short time we've known each other, we've shared some truly wonderful times. I'm craving to be with him again.

* * *

"What is this?" Holly asks as she picks up the piece of paper off the coffee table and reads it.

When I read the letter myself a few minutes ago, the news shocked me. It was the last thing I expected to see when I got home from work this evening.

"They're selling?!" Holly's surprise pretty much mimics my reaction.

"Apparently," I reply, faking a smile and rolling my eyes. I'm still trying to process all the different ways in which this news could potentially affect me.

"What does this mean?" she asks, setting the letter back down on the coffee table.

"Like it says, it all depends on who buys the building," I reply. "I may end up having to move... who knows?"

"I'm so sorry," Holly says, shaking her head. "You've lived here forever. I can't believe you might get evicted!"

"Hopefully, that's not the case," I say, although I have no idea what's going to happen now.

As soon as I read the letter saying the owners of this property have decided to sell, the first thought I had was that I'd have to move. This house is beautiful. Chances are the new owners will want to renovate the three separate units back into a one family home. None of the other houses on this street are multi-family homes, and anyone wanting a stunning, old Victorian in a great neighborhood is going to gobble this property up and renovate. It's just a feeling I have, and I could be wrong, but I have to prepare myself for the possibility of moving in the near future.

Suddenly, Holly audibly gasps and covers her mouth with her hand. "What?" I ask, searching the floor and coffee table for the huge spider I'm sure my arachnophobic sister just saw.

She looks at me, lowers her hand from her mouth, and says, "Maybe Patrick will buy this place!"

Okay, there's not a spider.

"Patrick?" I'm confused. Holly's boyfriend already owns The Pioneer, one of the most popular hotels in town. Why would he want to buy an apartment building, too?

She nods. "He was talking about wanting to buy some real estate. Something he could turn into a rental to make additional income. This is perfect!"

Her news surprises me. "That would be great!" Chances are, if Patrick bought this property and wants it for a rental, I wouldn't have to move anytime soon.

"I'm going to call him and let him know," she says as she walks down the hall toward her room.

As if on cue, my own phone rings. As soon as I look at the screen and see that it's Garrick, my face lights up in a smile. "Hi," I say as I answer the phone.

"Hey, babe. How was your day?"

I sigh. "Work was good. Then I came home and found a letter from my landlord saying they're putting this house on the market."

"Oh, no. Do you think you'll have to move?"

"I don't know," I reply. "I guess it depends on who they sell it to. Coincidentally, Holly's boyfriend is interested in buying a rental property, so she's calling him now to let him know. Maybe he'll end up buying it, and I'll get to stay."

"Hmmm. Well, things'll work out no matter what," Garrick says. "If you *do* end up having to move, maybe it's the universe's way of telling you to move to Oregon."

I laugh. I mean, he's joking, right?

Except he's not laughing.

"Ummm, what exactly would I do in Oregon?" I ask, trying to keep my voice light while my insides are all twisted up. Is he being serious?

"Last I checked, Oregon has libraries, which need librarians to work at them," he says, still without any laughter. "Plus, *I* live in Oregon, so that could be fun."

Not sure what to say to that, I laugh again. "Uh-huh... I'll keep that in mind." Surely, he can't be serious. We've known each other for less than two weeks. As much as I like him, I can't pack up and move my entire life hundreds of miles away to be with him.

"I mean, it would definitely be a risk," Garrick continues, and I still can't tell if he's joking or not. "But it may turn out to be worth it. You never know."

I'm not sure how to respond to that. Is he being serious?

I laugh again. "Well, we'll see what happens. Maybe Patrick will buy it, and I'll be able to stay here. Or maybe someone else will buy it, and I can still stay. Only time will tell. I'm going to try not to freak out too much."

"That's a good idea," he replies. "It's not worth stressing over something you have no control over."

"So, how was your day today?" I ask, wanting to change the subject.

"Pretty good. Nothing too crazy happened at the bookstore. It's getting to be crunch time for me to get ready for my trip, though. I'm doing laundry tonight, and tomorrow, I'll pack up all my things here at Sophie's house. I'm working tomorrow and Wednesday, then I'm heading back to my condo in Portland."

"I'm excited for you," I say, and it's true. Although I wish I could join Garrick on his trip, I hope he has an amazing time while he's there.

"It's not too late, you know," he says.

"For what?"

"To come with me." The way his deep, sexy voice says that gives me butterflies.

"I wish I could," I reply.

"Are you sure you can't?"

Damn.

I sigh. "Yeah, I am. I can't leave my job."

Garrick sighs as well. "Okay. You know I have to at least *try* to change your mind, though."

"Yeah... It's nice to know you want me to go with you."

"Of course I do," he says with sincerity in his voice. "I totally understand your position, though. It would be a huge sacrifice for you to drop everything in your life and travel halfway around the world with me." He chuckles, but something he said strikes a chord with me.

A huge sacrifice. My Tarot reading. Lorelei said I'd have to make a sacrifice to move on with my life. Could this be the sacrifice she was talking about? How will I know when I'm supposed to make that sacrifice—whatever it may be?

Trust your gut. He's worth it. Lorelei's words come flooding back, and my heart pounds. I'm not sure what to think now.

"You okay?" Garrick asks, and I realize I haven't said anything. I'm not even sure if he said something else after acknowledging it would be a huge sacrifice for me to go. My mind is spinning.

"Oh, yeah. Sorry, I spaced out for a second," I reply. I need to shove all these thoughts aside so I can finish this conversation with Garrick without being distracted.

But I definitely have a lot to think about later.

* * *

"Hi, girls!" Mom greets Holly and me as she opens the door.

"Hey, Mom," I say, giving her a hug before walking into my childhood home. Holly and I come over for dinner every Tuesday.

"Your dad's in the kitchen. Go on back there, and we'll open a bottle of wine," Mom says as she closes the door.

We all walk back to the kitchen, where Dad is stirring something in a pot on the stove. "Hi, girls," he says as we walk in.

"Hi, Dad. How are you?" I peer into the pot to see what he's cooking, and I'm happy to see his delicious alfredo sauce.

"I'm good. How are things going with you?" he asks.

"Oh, you know... the usual," I lie. My parents know nothing about Garrick or how I've been vacillating for the past twenty-four hours about whether I should pack up my life and run off to Australia with him for a month.

"That's not true," Holly pipes up, and my eyes shoot to her, standing on the other side of the counter. If she mentions Garrick's name, I'm going to kill her. I'm not ready to tell Mom and Dad about him yet. "Patrick might become Summer's new landlord."

"What?" Mom and Dad both say, clearly confused by what Holly said.

I relax a little now that Holly didn't bring up Garrick's name. "Yeah, I guess that's true," I say with a laugh.

"What do you mean?" Mom asks.

"Well, we got a letter in the mail saying the owners of the house are going to put the house on the market," Holly explains. "It just so happens that Patrick has been thinking about buying a rental property, so I told him about it right away, and he contacted a real estate agent about it!"

"Wow, that's exciting," Mom says, then selects a bottle of wine to open. She brings it over to the counter to open it, and as soon as I see the label, I do a double take.

Made in Australia.

Of all the wines Mom could've selected from her stash, she chose one from Australia. What are the chances? How many wines are actually made in Australia?

I don't know the answer to that... maybe a lot of wines are made there... but it's still the one place that has been at the forefront of my mind for the past forty-eight hours.

Is this some sort of sign?

Mom goes about opening the bottle and pours a glass for each of us.

"Thanks," I say as she hands me a glass. I take a sip. It's absolutely delicious. "This is good wine."

She and Holly both take sips and agree.

"I've never bought this kind before, but I saw the bottle and had to try it," Mom says, and I wonder what she means.

"Why's that?" Holly asks before I do.

Mom holds the bottle so we can see the label. "Look at how artistic it is! I love all the colors and the abstract couple kissing on it. I just found it intriguing for some reason."

"That *is* pretty," Holly says.

As I look at the label, which is one of the most beautiful pieces of art I've ever seen on a bottle of wine, I can't help but wonder if this truly is some sort of sign. A couple? Kissing? On a bottle of Australian wine? How can this be a simple coincidence?

Dad taps the wooden spoon he was stirring the sauce with against the pot. "Your mom and I have some news."

"You do?" Holly asks.

"What is it?" I wonder what it could possibly be.

Mom and Dad glance at one another and smile. "We're taking a trip," Mom says.

"It's something we've wanted to do for a long time, but we've put it off for years," Dad adds, and I wonder where they could be going. Mom and Dad haven't gone on a vacation for a few years.

"We're taking a cruise to Alaska!" The joy on Mom's face makes me smile, too.

"Wow! That's awesome," Holly says. We both know Mom has wanted to take a cruise to Alaska forever, so I'm excited she's finally getting the chance to go.

"When are you leaving?" I ask.

"In just a couple of weeks," Dad replies, which takes me by surprise.

"Two weeks?" Holly is clearly surprised, too. "That's soon!"

"Yeah, we found a good deal and decided to book it," Mom says.

"What about work and stuff?" Holly asks. Mom and Dad both still work—Dad has been at the paper mill for over thirty years, and Mom has been a bank teller for about fifteen years now. She was a stay-at-home mom with all of us girls until Holly was a teenager.

"We're taking time off," Mom says matter-of-fact.

Dad adds, "We both have vacation time to use, and we decided to go for it. It may be last minute, but we deserve this trip. It's been a long time coming, and we couldn't pass up such a good deal."

"That's awesome," I say, excited my parents are finally taking a well-deserved vacation.

"Sometimes, you just have to say *to hell with it* and do what's good for you, you know?" Mom adds, and her words hit me hard.

If this evening isn't a huge, flashing, billboard sign, telling me I should take a chance and go to Australia with Garrick, I don't know what it is.

Or, perhaps I'm making all these coincidences out to be something they're not.

As we eat dinner, Mom and Dad continue to tell us more about their upcoming cruise. Their excitement rubs off on me, and it makes me want to go to Australia even more.

Why does life have to be so unfair sometimes? As bad as I want to go, it's just not feasible right now. I have to work. I can't just leave all my responsibilities behind for a month. I can't let my emotions get the better of me.

"Are you okay, Summer?" Mom asks out of the blue.

"What? Yeah, why?"

"I don't know... you just seem distracted," Mom replies. "Is something on your mind?"

Holly nudges me with her knee, and I shoot her a glare, hoping Mom and Dad won't notice the subtle exchange between us. She better not mention anything about Garrick. I'll kill her if she does.

"I'm fine," I lie. "Really, I am."

"Okay," Mom replies, giving me the sort of smile that makes me think she doesn't fully believe me.

Shit. I don't need Mom's intuition to pick up on my personal life right now.

As Holly drives the two of us back home later, she catches me off guard when she says, "You should just go to Australia."

"What? Why?" I ask. Has she lost her mind?

"Because you clearly miss him."

I'm not sure what to say to that. She's right. I *do* miss Garrick, and it's only been a couple of days since he left. But flying halfway around the world and spending a month on another continent because I'm missing someone I've only known a couple of weeks is clearly insane.

"But I have a job," I say, explaining the rational reason of why I can't, in fact, go

with him. "I can't just drop everything and leave."

"Why not?"

I do a double-take at my younger sister in the driver's seat next to me. Has she

heard anything I've said? "Holly, I have a job. I have responsibilities. I can't go to Australia."

She sighs. "I know… but what an amazing adventure that would be. I know you'd be sacrificing a lot, though."

There's that word again. *Sacrifice.* I can't help but think about what Lorelei told me. Am I reading too much into all this?

I need to let this go. I'll see Garrick again when he returns from his trip. If it's meant to be, things will work out between us, and if it's not, things won't. I can't go to Australia, plain and simple, and I can't allow myself to keep obsessing over this.

Ugh! Being a responsible adult sucks sometimes.

Garrick

Chapter 13

I can't believe I'm leaving for Australia tomorrow.

Every time I get ready to leave for a trip, I feel anxious about what I'm forgetting to pack, or what piece of business I'm forgetting to take care of before leaving the country. The last couple of days before I take off are the worst in terms of anxiety and feeling as if I'm running out of time, so I'm in full-on panic mode now.

However, this time is different. I'm not only stressing about packing and being ready to go, but I also feel like I *am* leaving something behind—Summer.

I wish there was a way for her to join me on this trip. How incredible would it be to spend a month together, traveling around the continent of Australia? Yeah, it sounds crazy since we've only known each other a couple of weeks. But I don't care how it sounds. I know how I feel about Summer, and I know how she feels about me. Things have progressed quickly between us, and, no, I'm not *in love* with her yet... but I can see things going that way for us if our relationship continues in the direction we're going.

But now we're basically putting everything on hold. Sure, we can text, call, video call, even email each other while I'm gone, but it would be a million times better to hold her in my arms as we take a boat cruise under the Sydney Harbor Bridge.

Instead, I'll be taking in the sights all by myself.

Don't get me wrong—I enjoy traveling alone. I've done it dozens of times before, and I always have an incredible time. I've even made a career out of traveling by myself. I've wanted to visit Australia for years, and I'm finally going there. This is sure to be one of my best trips yet, and I'm looking forward to the articles I plan to write about the various sights I see.

My phone rings. I pick it up from my bedside table and instantly smile when I see Summer's name on the screen. "Hey, babe," I say when I answer.

"Hi! What are you up to?"

"Oh, just finishing laundry and packing. Getting ready to go. I can't believe I'm leaving tomorrow."

"Yeah, that's exciting," she says.

"I've been planning this trip for months, but I've wanted to go to Australia for years, so this feels a bit surreal, to be honest."

"I'm excited for you!"

"Thanks, babe. I'm looking forward to finally getting there. I'm *not* really looking forward to the long flight, though."

Summer laughs. "Yeah, that sounds torturous. Did you say it's eighteen hours?"

"Yep. I've never been on such a long flight before. Hopefully, it won't be too bad."

It would be better with you—is what I want to say, but I

don't. Summer can't go with me, and I don't want to make her feel bad about it. She's made it clear that she'd go if she could, but I understand she can't leave for a long vacation like this on such short notice.

"So, are you just hanging out at your condo all day, getting ready to go?" Summer asks.

"No, I'm going to my parents' house later to have dinner with them and to say goodbye. But other than that, I'll be home, getting ready for tomorrow."

"Cool," Summer says. "I'm sure your parents will be happy to see you before you're gone for a month."

"Yeah. It'll be good for me to see them, too. It's kind of hard to leave for such a long period of time."

"I'm sure it is," she says. "So, what time are you going over there? Or, rather, what time will you be back? I want to call you again tonight, but after you get home."

"Eh, I don't know... I'll probably be home around seven-thirty or eight, I guess."

"Okay," she says. "I'll call you around then."

"Are you saying goodbye to me already? You just called!"

"No." She laughs. "I just meant I'll call you *again* around that time. We can keep talking now."

"Okay, good. Because I like hearing your voice. And I like talking to you."

"Is that right?"

"Yeah, it is. In fact, I like it a lot," I tell her. "I like *you* a lot, Summer."

"Aww..." I swear I can hear Summer blushing through the phone.

As much as I'm looking forward to my trip tomorrow, it

seems to be a fraction less exciting since I'm leaving Summer behind.

* * *

After enjoying a delicious home-cooked meal at my parents' house, and their company, I'm on my way home. I don't have to get up early tomorrow, so I can sleep in a little. My flight doesn't leave until noon... and then my long day of travel begins. I have a layover in LA for two hours before continuing on to Sydney. I hate sleeping on planes, but at least I splurged for first class. Jet lag is going to be a bitch with the seventeen-hour time difference—*that's* for sure. It'll be nine o'clock on Saturday night when I finally arrive.

After I get home from my parents' house, I decide to chill out and watch TV for a while. My phone rings, and of course, it's Summer. She said she'd call around this time.

"Hey, babe. How are you?"

"Hi! I'm good... how was dinner with your parents?" she asks.

"It was nice. I'm glad I went over there to see them before my trip."

"That's good. So, um, can you do me a favor?" she asks, and I wonder what she's going to say.

"Are you going to ask me to bring you back a souvenir from Australia? I was already planning on it," I say with a chuckle. Hell, I've already planned on getting her something from each city I visit.

"No. I was going to ask if you could let me into your building."

Let her into my building? Does she want to come here while I'm out of town or something? Why would she—

"Garrick—" her voice interrupts my thoughts— "did you hear me? Can you buzz me in, please?"

Suddenly, it hits me. I shoot up from my couch like a rocket. "Wait, you're here right *now*?" I head toward my front door.

"Yeah," she says with a nervous laugh. "Surprise!" Her voice sounds a little timid, as if she's nervous.

Instead of buzzing her in, I rush out my door. "I'll be down in a minute," I tell her as I push the button for the elevator. "What—how—what are you doing here?" My heart pounds in my chest, excited to see Summer face to face in just a matter of minutes.

"I—I hope your offer still stands..."

The elevator arrives with a ding. "What?" I ask, not sure what she means. The elevator doors slide open, and I hurry on, pressing the button for the lobby, then repeatedly pressing the one for the doors to close. I say a silent prayer that it'll be a direct ride all the way down without having to stop at any other floors.

"To go to Australia with you," Summer says just as the doors slide closed. "I changed my mind, and I'm packed and ready to go with you."

As the elevator descends, my heart leaps to my throat. "Are you—are you serious?"

"Yeah. I hope it's not too late," she says. "I bought a ticket on the same flights as you last night and drove down to Autumn's house this afternoon. I'm sitting in her car with her right now outside your building."

Running my free hand through my hair, I'm stunned. She's going with me? She bought her own ticket? She's here, ready to go to Australia? I have so many questions, but I'm so fucking surprised and elated, I don't even know where to start.

And why is this elevator so slow? It seems to take twice as long to get to the lobby, even though I'm not stopping on any other floors.

"What made you change your mind?" I ask. I suppose that's a good place to start.

She laughs once, then replies, "Well, I decided to trust my gut for once. Even though it made absolutely no sense for me to leave everything and go with you, it was all I could think about. I was driving myself crazy, thinking about you going without me."

My smile widens, which, at this point, I didn't think was possible. "Holy shit. I can't believe you're really here. I'm on my way down in the elevator, by the way. I'll meet you outside in a minute."

The elevator finally comes to a stop and opens to the lobby. I rush off, running to the door to get outside. "Where are you parked?" I ask as I step out onto the sidewalk, looking up and down the street for her.

"Look to your left," she says.

I turn my head and see a car door open, and then Summer gets out. I run the short distance down the block to her. She smiles when she sees me, right before I wrap my arms around her and lift her off the ground. Summer squeals and laughs as I spin around in a circle.

I stop and slowly let her body slide down against mine

until her feet touch the ground. I take one look at her beautiful blue-green eyes, then crash my lips to hers in a searing-hot kiss. To have her in my arms right now is everything. I wished this would happen, for her to change her mind and travel with me, and now here she is, making my dream come true.

I savor her lips, not wanting to pull mine away, but we're out on the street, and I remember she said she was with her sister Autumn. Reluctantly, I slowly pull back, opening my eyes to her beautiful face and kissing her once more before forcing myself to stop. Her eyes flutter open, and she instantly smiles when she looks at me.

"Hi," she says, dazed.

"Hi," I reply, feeling dazed as well. I can't believe this is happening.

"So, it's okay if I go with you?"

I laugh. "Yes. Of course, it is. I'm beyond excited that you've decided to go with me."

We get lost in each other's eyes for a moment before I hear another person clear her throat. "Um, I'd hate to interrupt," the woman says, and both Summer and I turn to look at her. "Hi, I'm Summer's sister Autumn." The woman gives me a little wave, and I can see the resemblance between her and Summer. The only big difference between them is that Autumn's hair is darker brown than blond.

"Hi. It's nice to meet you," I say, stepping toward Autumn with my hand outstretched.

She shakes my hand and smiles. "It's nice to meet you, too. You better watch after my little sister while you're in Australia, okay?" We drop our hands. "I know where you live now," she adds with a wink.

I laugh. "You have nothing to worry about. Summer will be safe with me. I promise." I look at Summer to my left and wrap my arm around her waist.

Summer smiles back at me. "Don't worry, you'll be safe with me, too," she says with a laugh.

Autumn pops her trunk, and I help Summer remove her luggage. She has two suitcases, plus a backpack, and I take them all to the sidewalk. "Do you want to come up with us?" I ask Autumn.

"No, no, I'm parked in a loading zone, so I should get going," she says. Then, she hugs her sister. I can hear them talking, but I can't make out what they're saying. It's nice to see how close Summer is with her sisters. Now that I've met two of them, I can tell she has a close-knit family.

They end their hug, and Summer says to Autumn, "I'll let you know when we arrive in LA tomorrow."

"Keep me posted throughout your trip," Autumn says, then she looks at me again. "It was nice to meet you, Garrick. Have fun!"

"It was a pleasure meeting you, too," I say. "And we will have a great time. Don't worry."

Autumn smiles at us, then walks around to the driver's side of her car. She waves and says goodbye one more time before getting in and shutting the door.

I turn to Summer. "Let's go inside."

I insist on taking her suitcases for her, and we make our way up to my condo. Once inside, I wrap my arms around her again. "I can't believe you're here."

"I know. It's crazy, right?"

"How did you make this happen?" I ask, curious how she

got the time off work after all. "Let's sit, and you can explain everything."

We sit on the couch next to each other, but I want her closer. "Come here," I say, moving into the corner of the couch so she can sit between my legs with her back to my front. She moves and leans back against me as I wrap my arms around her. I kiss her cheek, then ask, "What did your boss say when you said you're taking a month off?"

"Well... I sorta quit," she says, and I whip my head forward to look at her.

"You what?!"

She nods. "I know, it's insane. I loved my job. But I also couldn't pass up this opportunity."

"You just up and quit? Were they mad?" I can't believe she made the ultimate sacrifice and quit her job so she could travel with me.

"No, not really," she says. "I mean, yes, they were upset that I decided to leave, but they were also happy for me. I've worked there a long time, and it turns out that by me leaving, it opened up the opportunity for another employee to go full time, which is something she has been wanting to do. So, I actually made someone else's dream come true, which made me more at ease with my decision."

"Well, that worked out well," I say, still shocked by her news. "What are you going to do when you get back?"

Summer shrugs. "I don't know. I'll figure it out then. My boss actually told me she'd rehire me when I return, although it might be part time for a while."

I kiss her cheek again, then lean my head against hers. "I can't believe you did this. But I'm so glad you did." Then, another thing she said comes to mind. "And you bought your plane tickets? That must've cost you a fortune! I'll reimburse you—"

"No, no," she says. "You don't have to do that. I had some money in my savings account that I used to pay for them."

"But tickets to Australia aren't cheap, especially at the last minute like this. Let me help. You wouldn't even be going if it weren't for me."

"No, really, Garrick. Let me pay for my own ticket."

Wow, she's stubborn. I get it, though. She wants to pay her own way. I'm sure she bought a ticket in coach, though. Hopefully, there's still space in first class, and I can pay for her upgrade when we arrive at the airport tomorrow.

"What about your apartment?" I ask as more questions spring to my mind.

"Instead of Holly moving out into Patrick's apartment at the hotel right away, they're going to stay at our place while I'm gone. He's trying to negotiate a price to buy the building, too."

"That's awesome," I say, glad everything ended up working out for her to come with me.

I kiss her cheek again. Then behind her ear. *God, she smells good*. I kiss her neck, and she squirms a bit between my legs.

"That tickles," she whispers, but she also sounds turned on.

I keep going, kissing her everywhere I can reach from this angle, my hands sliding up her body to her breasts. Summer lets out a moan, causing my dick to harden.

"I want you," I say, nibbling on her ear.

"I want you, too," she says.

"Turn around. Ride my cock," I whisper in her ear, causing her to squirm again.

She turns her head so I can kiss her, briefly, and then she stands, turning around to face me. Seductively, Summer strips for me, slowly shimmying out of her clothes, turning me on while also driving me crazy. I'm craving her, and while I enjoy her wanting to be sexy for me, taking her time to remove her clothes, I also can't wait for her to be naked.

As she unhooks her bra and slides it off, I sit up and pull off my own shirt. She smirks, then runs her hands over the waistband of her pink, lacy underwear. I reach for the fly of my jeans and undo my pants, then stand to take them off. Summer watches me with hooded eyes as she teases me by not taking her panties off yet. I drop my jeans to the floor, then proceed to take off my boxer briefs. My cock springs free, ready for her. She bites her bottom lip, keeping eye contact with me as she finally slides her underwear down, then tosses them to the floor.

My mouth goes dry as I look at her. She's gorgeous; everything I've ever wanted in a woman, and she's mine. I have the next month to show her how much she means to me... how much I'm falling in love with her.

Fuck. I need her. I reach for her and pull her toward me as I sit back down on the couch. She straddles me, cradling my head in her hands as she crashes her lips to mine. Summer wants to take this slow, but I'm dying to be buried deep inside her. I move my hand between her legs and find her clit, rubbing it in circles. She bucks her hips forward and moans in my mouth. She's already so wet, she could just sit on my dick and slide right in...

But I know she needs more first. I adjust my hand, sliding two fingers inside her while continuing to rub her clit with my thumb. She moans again and moves her hips against my hand. She pulls her lips away from mine, her head falling back and her chest arching toward me. Her taut nipples are just inches from my face, so I lean forward a bit to give one attention with my tongue.

"Yes, just like that," Summer moans, and her hand glides up her body to fondle her other breast.

I pleasure her nipple with my mouth while my fingers get her closer to release. I can tell she's almost there, so I lightly bite down on her puckered nipple.

"Yes!" she calls out, bucking her hips harder. I flick it a few times with my tongue before biting it again, and suddenly, she comes undone. "God! Yes!" Summer soaks my fingers and rides out her orgasm until she slows to a stop. Her eyes open, and she looks at me, a slow smile spreading on her lips. "I want your cock," she says, reaching between us and taking it in her hand. She strokes it a few times before leaning in and whispering in my ear, "I'm on the pill."

Realizing she means I don't need to use a condom, I smile back at her. "Ride my cock. Please."

She smirks before adjusting her body, sliding down onto me. My head falls back against the couch. God, she feels incredible. She glides up and down, raking her fingernails across my chest. Her pussy is so wet, so tight, I know I'm not going to last long. I lift my head to watch her, and the sight of her body riding me, her breasts bouncing, and how beautiful she looks doing it is the sexiest thing I've ever seen.

I don't want to come before her, so I move my hand between us and find her clit again. Rubbing in circles, it doesn't take long before her muscles clench around my cock, and she calls out in pleasure. The way her pussy grips my cock sets me off as well, and I grit my teeth as my head falls back against the couch.

I'm not sure how long it takes us to recover, but Summer stays where she is, straddling me for a while as we both calm down. I'm overflowing with emotions. My feelings for Summer are unlike anything I've ever experienced. She's nothing like the other women I dated in my past. She's smart, fun, independent, and to top it all off, sexy as hell. My attraction to her is stronger than anything I've ever felt before, and it suddenly occurs to me that I'm not *falling* in love. I'm already there.

Eventually, she stands and begins gathering her clothes off the floor. I watch her move, and I can't help myself. I blurt out, "I love you."

Summer stops. She's kneeling on the floor, picking up her pants. She stands, turning to face me. Her mouth opens, then closes again, as if she's not sure what to say. Then, her lips curl upward. "Did you just say what I think you said?"

I nod. "I love you, Summer."

She drops the clothes in her hands. "You do?" she asks, and I notice her eyes have tears in them.

I stand and walk over to her. Placing my hands on her shoulders, I look into her eyes. "Yes, I do. I've been falling for you since the day we met. The fact that you quit your job and dropped everything just to travel with me confirmed my feelings, though. I'm in love with you."

A tear falls from her eye, and Summer quickly wipes it away. "I love you, too, Garrick."

I wrap my arms around her, holding her close. It's crazy how quickly everything has happened between Summer and me, but I'm so grateful I met her. Tomorrow, we start our first adventure together, and I plan on making it extra special for her. She deserves the world, and I plan on spoiling her with everything it has to offer... starting with Australia.

Summer

Chapter 14

"Oh, my God! I can't believe how beautiful this is!"

I've said this same sentence countless times over the past three weeks. Australia has been absolutely breathtaking. We've worked our way up the eastern coast, from Sydney to Brisbane to Cairns, and everywhere in between. Australia has completely outdone my expectations so far, but the beautiful sight in front of me now is the most stunning view I've ever seen in my life.

Garrick wraps his arms around me from behind as the catamaran we're traveling on gets closer to the Great Barrier Reef. It may be winter here in the southern hemisphere, but the weather in this part of the country feels like summer. Sydney and Brisbane were colder and rainier, similar to a mild Pacific Northwest winter, but the further north we traveled, the warmer it got.

The same can be said about Garrick and me. We've only become closer over the course of this trip. I feel thankful every morning I wake up beside him that he invited me to join him. I'm also extremely grateful I chose to take a chance and follow my heart. That Lorelei was right—it was a huge sacrifice to quit my job, but I haven't regretted it one second. She was also right about Garrick—he's played an important role in my life, and he's nothing like other guys I've dated in the past. Trusting my gut has definitely been worth it, just like she told me it would be.

"Look at that," Garrick says, pointing out in the distance, and I see the majestic scene just in time. A whale breaches, coming back down on the water with a huge splash.

"That's amazing!" I practically squeal like a little girl.

"Yeah, it is," Garrick agrees right before we see a second whale do exactly the same thing.

We both gasp. There are others on the boat gathering near us as well, taking in the incredible sight. Garrick takes out his phone and snaps a few pictures.

It's been interesting watching him work on this trip. He captures everything he wants to remember in pictures and keeps detailed notes on his phone to remind him of all the things he wants to write about later. He spends every evening writing for an hour or more. It's a nice, relaxing time for me. I usually spend the time checking in with my family and friends or looking at social media. Then, Garrick lets me read what he wrote, which I thoroughly enjoy as well. He always asks for my opinion on his writing, and he says he appreciates me helping proofread his work.

Yesterday, when I talked to Holly, she let me know that the offer Patrick made on our building has been accepted! This is great news, and I feel relieved that I won't be kicked out of my apartment anytime soon. However, now that Garrick and I have been together twenty-four seven for the past three weeks, I'm dreading having to say goodbye to him when we return home. We haven't talked about the logistics of our long-distance relationship yet.

Last week, Garrick introduced me to his parents via Zoom. It was interesting to meet his mom and dad over a video call, but it was still nice. His parents were very kind and eager to meet me. At the end of the call, they said they can't wait to meet me in person, and they hope it's sooner rather than later.

My parents were also eager to meet the man I ran away with. Back home, when I broke the news to them that I was going to Australia, they both nearly had heart attacks. I made Holly come along with me when I told them, just so she could verify that Garrick was a good man, not a serial killer. Her presence didn't seem to help at all, though.

Mom and Dad were pretty mad at me for not telling them about Garrick prior to that moment, especially when they found out he had visited me in Port Townsend just days before. I was in trouble, and I felt bad for hurting them, but at the time, I didn't think it was the right time to introduce Garrick to my parents yet. I had no idea how quickly our feelings for each other would evolve into something more, or that I would end up making the decision to go on this trip with him.

Needless to say, I had a lot of explaining to do. In the end, they still weren't okay with me flying halfway around the world with Garrick, but they knew they couldn't stop me. Since I was planning to surprise Garrick with my plan to join him, I couldn't have my parents talk to him yet, but I did leave them with the name, address, and phone number of his sister's bookstore in Seaside, as well as the web address to

Garrick's travel blog. That seemed to help calm their nerves a little, but they were still uneasy with the situation.

As soon as we arrived in Australia, I called my parents to let them know we arrived, and Garrick talked to them for the first time then. When we finally had our Zoom call, and they got to see each other's faces on the screen, my parents were more at ease. They like Garrick, and they're comfortable with me being here with him now. They're also looking forward to meeting him in person sometime soon.

The catamaran slows down, and the captain makes an announcement that we've reached the spot for snorkeling. Garrick takes me by the hand and leads me to the other end of the boat, away from all the other passengers. We look over the railing into the water and see the unbelievably clear blue water below. A few fish swim beneath the surface. I'm mesmerized by it, and I still can't believe I'm actually here.

"This is incredible," Garrick says.

"Yeah, it is," I agree.

"No, I don't mean this," he says, and I look at him, wondering what he's talking about. "I mean *us*." He points between us, then continues, "Our relationship is incredible, Summer. *You're* incredible. I never expected my life to change the day you walked into Sophie's bookstore."

Oh. My heart pounds in my chest as I listen to Garrick's words. "I know things are moving at hyper speed between us—"

"You could say that," I interrupt, and we both laugh.

Garrick shakes his head. "I just love you, Summer. You make me feel good. You make me laugh. We've had an amazing time together on this trip, and you're a great travel partner! I can't believe we haven't had one fight this entire time. You're so easy to be around."

"I feel the same way about you," I tell him. "I've never had a relationship where everything just worked out together so well. *We* work together so well."

Garrick smiles. "That's exactly what I was thinking, too. It's like you fill this void in my life that I didn't realize was missing. I mean, I was fine before I met you, but now I can't imagine not having you in my life."

My heart swells with emotion. "I feel the same," I say.

Garrick takes one of my hands in his, and my heart races as he gets down on one knee. *Holy shit! Is this really happening right now?!*

I'm not prepared for this. We're standing on a catamaran in the Great Barrier Reef—the most beautiful place I've ever been—and Garrick is *proposing?!*

"Summer," he says, his other hand pulling something out of his pocket. "I know this is fast, but I can't imagine living my life without you. I wanted to make this vacation memorable for you—and me—and I couldn't think of a more romantic place to ask you... will you do me the honor of becoming my wife?"

My free hand flies to my chest. "Oh, my God," I whisper, my eyes stinging with tears.

"We can have a long engagement," Garrick adds. "I just don't want to go another day not knowing if you'll be by my side for the rest of our lives."

The tears fall, and I wipe them away. Garrick stands and helps wipe them as well. I look at the man I love and instantly nod my head. "Yes. Yes, of course I'll marry you, Garrick." Garrick smiles as he slides the diamond ring on my finger. It's beautiful. Something I would've picked out for myself. Garrick knows me well. "I love this," I say, admiring my beautiful engagement ring. I wasn't expecting this to happen so soon, but at the same time, this is absolutely perfect.

"I hoped you would," he replies. "I saw it in a jewelry store window right by our hotel in Brisbane, and I knew immediately that it had to be yours."

He bought this in Brisbane? How? When? We were always together!

He goes on to explain. "Our last morning there, while you were in the shower, I ran down to the jewelry store and bought it. I didn't know when I would give it to you. I honestly didn't plan on proposing right away. I wasn't even sure if I'd do it on this trip or wait until we got back home. But last night, I realized that today had to be the day. I had to ask you here in the middle of the Great Barrier Reef, on the other side of the Pacific from where we first met in Seaside."

I wrap my arms around his neck and kiss him. I love this man, and he loves me. I'm going to be his wife. *His wife!* I never imagined things would turn out this way between Garrick and me, and still, somehow, I always knew he was the one for me.

"Come on now," Garrick says. "Let's go snorkeling."

* * *

"It's so nice to finally meet you!" Mom gushes as she gives Garrick a hug. He's finally meeting my parents in person, and Mom and Dad are over the moon excited about it.

Mom lets go of him, and Dad shakes Garrick's hand. "It's a pleasure to meet you, Garrick. Can I get you a beer?"

"Sure, I'll have whatever kind you have," Garrick replies.

We walk into the living room to sit. I haven't broken the news of our engagement yet, and I'm trying to keep my left hand out of view. We returned from Australia five days ago. After we flew back to Portland, we spent the next day and a half at Garrick's condo, trying to acclimate from the jet lag. Then, we went to his parents' house for dinner, and I finally got to meet his mom and dad in person. We shared the big news with them, and they were elated. Garrick's mom is already sending me wedding ideas via text.

Now, it's time to tell my folks. We arrived in Port Townsend last night, and now we're here to have dinner with my parents. To say I'm nervous is an understatement. Sure, they like Garrick, but I'm not sure how they'll take this news. It's extremely soon for us to be engaged under normal circumstances, but I wouldn't consider our relationship to be completely normal. After all, we just spent a month in Australia together after only knowing each other for a couple of weeks.

Of course, I already shared the news with my sisters. They're all excited for us, and Sophie is happy for us, too. I feel guilty for not telling my parents right away, but I wanted them to meet Garrick first, and I also wanted to tell them in person. This is the first chance we've had to do that.

"Tell us about your trip," Mom says as Dad goes into the kitchen for drinks. "I mean, I know we talked multiple times while you were there, but I want to know all about it!"

I laugh. I don't want to wait to tell them we're engaged. I tell her a few things about Australia while we wait for Dad to return to the room. As soon as he comes back, he hands Garrick a beer, then sits in his recliner with his own drink.

"So, we have something exciting to share with you," I say, and Mom and Dad look at us, expectantly. Nerves take over, and I have butterflies. Hopefully, my parents take the news as well as everyone else has so far. "Well, we know it's fast, but..." I hold my left hand up so they can see the diamond ring adorning my ring finger.

Mom gasps, and her hands fly to her face in shock. "Oh, my—" She stands and walks over to me, taking my hand with hers to examine my sparkling engagement ring.

Dad hasn't said anything, and now I'm worried. I look over at him, sitting in his chair, looking at me as if I just told him he has two heads. "What did you say?" he asks, and I suddenly feel like I'm going to throw up all of those butterflies in my stomach.

"Um—" I start to say, but then Mom holds my hand out for Dad to see.

"Look at this gorgeous ring, honey!"

Then, all of a sudden, Dad's face breaks into a smile. He stands and walks across the room to Garrick. "Nice job, man," Dad says, shaking Garrick's hand and patting him on the back. "Sorry, I tried to act surprised, but I think I freaked her out. I'm not the best actor."

Garrick chuckles. "No worries. I didn't want to drag it out too long anyway."

Confusion washes over me, and I pull my hand back from Mom. "Wait. What are you two talking about?" I ask Dad and Garrick.

They both chuckle. "Well, Summer," Dad says. "The truth is, Garrick called me from Australia to ask for my blessing before he popped the question."

My mouth drops open, and I look from Garrick to my dad, back to Garrick again. "You did what?"

Garrick shrugs his shoulder. "I didn't feel right proposing to you without asking your dad first, so the day before I bought the ring, I called him while you were in the shower."

I'm shocked. Here I thought we were going to surprise my parents, and I'm the one who's stunned. I don't know what to say.

"Congratulations, honey," Mom says.

I look at her in disbelief. "Did you already know, too?"

She nods. "Yeah. Garrick asked your dad to put me on speakerphone and asked us both. Of course, we were a little apprehensive since we barely know Garrick, but we also know how happy you are. We figured it was up to you anyway, and if you said yes, of course we'd give you our blessing."

Tears spring to my eyes. I stand and hug my mom. "Thank you."

"For what, honey?" she asks as we embrace.

"For being so supportive."

"Of course," she says as we drop our arms. "Plus, we've grown to love Garrick." She walks over to hug him as well. "Welcome to the family!"

Dad walks over and gives me a hug. "Congratulations, honey. You have a good guy here."

"Thank you," I say, wiping the tears from my eyes.

And that's the truth. I love Garrick, and I'm excited for what the future holds for us.

We won't even have to worry about living so far apart from each other, either. I made the decision to move to Portland with him. Holly and Patrick are going to move into our apartment, which he'll be the owner of soon anyway. It'll give them more living space than the small apartment he lives in now. I love Garrick's condo, so it wasn't too difficult for me to decide to move. This way, I'll also live closer to Autumn, which I'm excited about as well.

Yesterday, before we drove here to Port Townsend, I stopped at a local bookstore down the street from Garrick's condo that had a "now hiring" sign in the window. Sure, it's not the library, but it's an amazing bookstore within walking distance of his building. I talked with the owner, and she hired me on the spot. I start next week after we return to Portland again.

Everything is falling into place. Taking a chance and making a sacrifice was one of the most difficult decisions— and gambles—I've ever made in my life, but everything is coming together now.

I look at Garrick, my fiancé. He smiles, then mouths *I love you.*

Without a doubt in my mind, I know deep in my heart, he's my forever love.

The End

Also by C.L. Collier

Seasons of Love Series

Holly

Autumn

April

Summers in Seaside Series

Summer Magic - read Olivia and Stone's story, and more of the
lovable Lorelei at the Sandy Shore Inn!

Hot Vegas Nights Series

Playing Vegas

The Salvation Society

Harbor

The Vagabond Series

Passion in Paris

Belize Bliss

What I Never Knew Series

What I Never Knew

What I Never Knew I Wanted

What I Never Knew I Needed

Discovering Us Series

Stacking the Deck

Finding Our Rhythm

Worthy of Love

Meant to Be

Visit C.L. Collier's web site

Other books coming soon from C.L. Collier:

Stud Finder: A Limited Edition Romance Anthology - coming February 6, 2024

The Summers in Seaside Series

Thank you for reading Summer Love!

For more brand new stories filled with sun, sand and summer adventures that will tug at your heartstrings, check out the rest of the Summers in Seaside Series.

Grab the rest of the 2023 stories here:

Summer Escape by Amy Stephens

Second Chance Summer by Sascha Illyvich

The Summer Ultimatum by Amanda Shelley

A Sun-kissed Summer by M Leigh Morhaime

Hook, Line, and Summer by Tina Gallagher

Summer With My Sexy Ex by Denise Wells

Summer Nights by Mel Walker

One Summer Knight by Monica Misho-Grems

Taking Summer by Cassandra Cripps - read the story about the crying girl Summer saw at the Sandy Shore Inn!

Sweets of Summer by Barb Shuler & KA Graham

The Summer He Found Her by Rachel Radner

The Boys of Summer by Hope Irving

For books in the previous seasons, check out:

https://amandashelley.com/summers-in-seaside-series/

Consider joining our Reader's group to stay up to date with future releases:

https://www.facebook.com/groups/166945398852346

Acknowledgments

Thank you for reading *Summer Love*! I hope you enjoyed Summer and Garrick's story as much as I enjoyed writing it.

I love being a part of the Summers in Seaside Series, and I love that I was able to combine this book with my other new series, Seasons of Love. *Holly* is the first book in Seasons of Love, and her story is a short novella. Autumn's story will be coming out next, which will be included in the *Love and Coffee* anthology, and *April* will be released on April 1, 2024!

Once again, Amanda Shelley, thank you for being a great friend – my writing bestie! You're always there when I need to vent or get advice, and I truly appreciate you! I'm so glad you thought up the Summers in Seaside Series. How fun it's been to work together, and I'm looking forward to 2024!

Finally, if you read the dedication page at the beginning of this book, you saw that I dedicated it to my daughter. Both of my kids are growing up to be pretty awesome people, and I'd like to acknowledge them both here. My son is going into his senior year of high school this fall, and my daughter is going to be a freshman. Time really does go by *too* fast, and it seems like only yesterday they were babies. I can't wait to see how much they grow this coming year and where life ends up taking them. I know they'll both do incredible things in their futures!

Thanks again for reading!

About the Author

C.L. Collier lives in the beautiful Pacific Northwest. She was raised in the Seattle area, and although she lives closer to Portland, Oregon now, she frequently visits the hometown she loves. When she's not writing, you can find her reading, watching her favorite sports teams, spending time with her family, or going to concerts. She likes her music loud, wine and coffee sweet, and her books steamy.

Click here to visit CL Collier's web site!